a.k.a. Genius

a.k.a. genius

By Marilee Haynes

Pauline
BOOKS & MEDIA
Boston

Library of Congress Cataloging-in-Publication Data

Haynes, Marilee.

a.k.a. genius / by Marilee Haynes.

pages cm

Summary: "When standardized test scores identify seventh-grader Gabe Carpenter as St. Jude's resident genius, he wonders what it means to have brains when he can't even manage to open his own locker"– Provided by publisher.

ISBN-13: 978-0-8198-0830-1

ISBN-10: 0-8198-0830-X

[1. Genius–Fiction. 2. Self-esteem–Fiction. 3. Science projects–Fiction. 4. Catholic schools–Fiction. 5. Middle schools–Fiction. 6. Schools–Fiction.] I. Title.

PZ7.H3149146Aak 2013

[Fic]–dc23

2013009903

The Scripture quotations contained herein are from the New Revised Standard Version Bible: Catholic Edition, copyright © 1989, 1993, Division of Christian Education of the National Council of the Churches of Christ in the United States of America. Used by permission. All rights reserved.

Book design by Mary Joseph Peterson, FSP

Cover art by Tracy Hill

Published by Pauline Books & Media, 50 Saint Pauls Avenue, Boston, MA 02130-3491

Printed in U.S.A.

AKAG VSAUSAPEOILL4-10J13-03330 0830-X

www.pauline.org

Pauline Books & Media is the publishing house of the Daughters of St. Paul, an international congregation of women religious serving the Church with the communications media.

1 2 3 4 5 6 7 8 9   16 15 14 13

For my wonderful husband, Frank,

and our three precious gifts

—Charlie, Sara, and Anna.

I love you.

One

I clomp up the steps and through the front door, thinking about the squeak that followed me home. Well, followed me home because it's coming from the wheels of the backpack I was pulling behind me. The fact that it's definitely a squeak and not a squeal and that it happens at regular intervals—once per rotation—makes me sure I can take care of it with a little oil.

Once inside, I kick off my shoes and place them neatly in the basket by the front door, because that's what you do in my house. My mom has a "no-shoes-in-the-house" rule that you don't mess with. She also has a "don't-eat-cookies-in-your-bedroom" rule, but I think of that one as more of a suggestion. My plan is to snag a couple cookies and head to my room.

I've only taken 2¾ steps toward the kitchen when an itchy feeling like somebody's watching me starts between my shoulder blades. I swivel my head to the right and look into the dining room—nothing—then to the left. And there, sitting on the living room couch, are my parents.

This is weird for a couple reasons. First, it's the middle of the afternoon, and my dad should be at work. And second, no one sits on the living room couch. Heck, no one ever even goes into the living room. But there they are. In the living room. Sitting on the couch. Looking at me.

"Hi, Mom. Hi, Dad." If I act natural and just keep walking, maybe whatever the weird thing is can't touch me.

"Gabe, honey, come sit down," says my mom. The line between her eyebrows doesn't go with the smile on her face. "We need to talk to you about something." It looks like the weird thing is coming my way.

I search around in my brain and try to figure out what I did wrong or how I messed up. I come up blank. Nothing out of the ordinary has happened the last few days, my room is kind of picked up, and I did my homework last night. I don't even think I've been too rotten to my sister lately.

"What's going on?" I flop into the chair that's the only other place to sit. Too late, I remember this is not a chair for flopping. I wince and rub the spot on my butt that hit first.

"Well, Champ, Mr. Dooley called today and told your mom something interesting," says my dad.

Everyone knows that nothing good has ever happened to a kid after a call from the principal. My stomach clenches up like a fist. I hold myself perfectly still and wait for more.

"Do you remember those tests that you took at the beginning of the year?" my mom asks.

"Yeah, the whole seventh grade took them. It was two days of boring. What about them? Did I do something wrong?" They seemed pretty easy, but maybe I used the wrong kind of pencil or filled in the wrong bubbles.

"No," says my mom. "Just the opposite. It seems that you did exceptionally well." She stops and looks at my dad. My dad jerks his chin toward me, which I guess means he wants my mom to tell me.

"It seems that the tests showed that you have a very high IQ." My mom smoothes her already-smooth blonde hair. "Actually your IQ is so high that you're—"

"A genius! A real genius," my dad blurts. "What do you think about that?" He looks excited, like he thinks I won something. Any minute he's going to jump up and try to high five me.

What do I think about that? A genius? That can't be right. I mean I've always been pretty smart. I get good grades, and I like learning new things, especially science things. But a genius?

"I don't understand. I'm a genius? Really?" I don't understand what's happening. Which is funny, because if I'm a genius, I probably should understand.

A choking sound from around the corner makes us all jump.

"Sabrina?" says my mom. "Is that you? Are you all right?"

My sister comes out of her hiding place. Usually a champion eavesdropper, her cover is blown. She's coughing, and her eyes are watering.

"A bite of cookie went down the wrong way. What did you say, Dad? Gabe's a genius?" Sabrina looks at me and snorts. More coughing and watering. "No way is the shrimp a genius."

Sabrina is one year and four days younger but two inches taller than me. It's the taller part she never lets me forget.

"Sabrina, this doesn't concern you. You are not to tell anyone," says my mom.

"Please, Sabrina. Don't say anything," I say. She turns and studies me. "Please."

"Okay, okay, I won't." And I almost believe her. But before she leaves the room, she smirks a smirk that lets me know that is not what's going to happen. No way is she keeping this a secret.

"Do you have any questions?" my dad asks. "About what it means to be a genius?" He can't seem to stop saying the word. Or smiling.

Questions? Yeah, I have questions. Is this going to change anything? Is this going to change everything? Is it going to be better? Or will it make things even worse? But none of these are questions I can ask my mom and dad.

I chew on my lip and pull at a loose thread on my sock. Just that word, "genius," makes me feel different, like I'm not me anymore. The top of my head starts tingling, and my stomach goes queasy. The kind of queasy like when you're not sure if you want to get on the tallest, fastest roller coaster at the amusement park. Because if you do, you might get the ride of your life. Or you might throw up all over the person in front of you. It feels like that.

Two

Breathe in, breathe out, and go: 34 right, 4 left, 16 right. Listen for the click and lift. Nothing. It doesn't open. Again. I rest my forehead on the cool, green metal of my locker for almost no time at all. But it's long enough.

"Can't open it again, huh, genius?" says a voice behind me.

I straighten up, turn around, and face her. Sabrina.

"It's fine."

"So you're supposed to be a genius, but you still can't open your locker? Maybe Mom and Dad should have you retested." She laughs at her own stupid joke and then stands up as straight as she can and looks down her nose at me. "Have a great day, *little* brother."

I grab the handle of my rolling backpack and head to my first class of the day dragging all of my books behind me. All of my books, since I can't get into my locker to put any of them away. Again.

St. Jude Middle School is shaped like a U. My locker is at one end of the U, and my class is all the way at the other end, which means I have to make two left turns to get there. And for reasons I can't explain, I can only steer my backpack with my right arm. So I worry that my right arm is going to end up being longer than my left. Like when a tennis player has a muscle in one arm that's way bigger than the muscle in his other arm. Not that I have muscles, because I don't. Just one arm that might be longer than the other. Which would make me an even bigger freak. A genius with uneven arms.

Maybe it's because I'm thinking about my arms that it takes a minute for me to notice. As I walk past kids still standing at their lockers, a few of them point or stare at me. Some of them are whispering. A girl I don't know says, "That's him. That's the genius." Someone else says, "Hey, Einstein," and snickers.

I feel my ears get hot, and I accidentally run the wheels of my backpack into the heel of my right foot.

Sabrina worked even faster than I thought she would. Popularity is practically a business at St. Jude, and information is its currency. And since being popular is Sabrina's ultimate goal, she doesn't care if it's *my* information she's trading for it.

My information. They're talking about me. Which means there's been a complete system breakdown. Before middle school started, I worked out a survival strategy that had as its most important component one simple thing: not getting noticed. Not getting talked about. Not calling attention to myself.

I pretend not to see the stares or hear the whispers. The only thing I can think to do is look down and keep walking. I wish I had a hat or something to hide behind. But when you have hair like mine, a hat is not your friend. My hair is like a brown helmet that sits on my head and doesn't do anything except get fuzzy when it rains or if it's humid. It's my own no-tech weather machine.

My history class is still two rooms away when I hear someone yell, "Hey, Gabe! Wait up."

It's my best friend, Linc. Well, Lincoln Jefferson Truman, but he goes by Linc. His parents have big plans for him, and I guess they thought naming him after three presidents might help. I'm not so sure.

"Hey. So, I heard something crazy before school even started." Linc shoots me a sideways look from under his pile of white-blond hair. He always looks like he needs a haircut.

"Yeah, what'd you hear?" I'm sure it's about me. But since Sabrina is the reason I'm today's headline, the story could have turned into anything by now.

"I heard you're a genius. Isn't that funny?" Linc starts laughing. Hard. Then he stops walking and looks at me. "You're not laughing. Why aren't you laughing? Is it true?" The questions keep coming. "Oh my gosh, you are. You're a genius."

Linc doesn't seem to need me for this conversation so I keep walking, and rolling.

"No, stop. Tell me," says Linc. "Tell me what's going on."

"I don't really know. Mr. Dooley told my mom and dad that I got a high score on those tests we took at the beginning of the year." I shrug. I'm still confused by all of it.

"Why didn't anyone know before? Have you always been a genius?" asks Linc. "And what happens now?" That's the first question he's asked that I have an answer for.

"So far it looks like my mom expects me to get even better grades. And starting tomorrow I'm in some new enrichment class that will help me 'reach my true potential.'" I roll my eyes.

There was a lot of talk about my potential last night. It was decided (not by me) that I haven't been fulfilling mine. Luckily for me, tomorrow starts a new quarter so I can get going on this potential thing right away.

"None of that sounds good," says Linc. "Wait, did you say there's going to be a new enrichment class?" I nod. "Oh man, I hope my mom doesn't find out. You know she'll try to get me in even if I don't belong." Linc frowns, which looks out of place on his face. But he should worry. His mom has a way of finding things out and making things happen. Whether Linc wants them to or not.

We walk into history class and sit in our usual seats. After the sixth person asks me if I'm really a genius, I put my head down on my desk and pretend to sleep. Linc laughs and throws wads of paper at my head until class starts.

Mrs. Rockmeyer gives back the tests we took last week. When I get mine, I see that I got a B, which is what I usually get in history. I also see a note next to the B that says, "Gabe, I'll be expecting more from you." Great. History isn't that interesting, so I don't spend much time on it. But it looks like Bs aren't going to be good enough anymore.

Only one more class to go, and the only person who hasn't acted like I'm a freak today is Linc. If I hear the word "genius" one more time, I might start screaming. But if I start screaming, I won't be able to stop. And then

I'll be the crazy genius and even more people will stare at me and talk about me.

I put my head down and walk as fast as I can to meet Maya. She wasn't in the cafeteria during lunch even though it was sausage biscuit day—her favorite. It's weird that I haven't seen her all day. We meet at the Saint Jude statue and go to geometry together every day.

I get to the statue first, which never happens. Maybe it's because I was walking so fast. It's the perfect place to be invisible for a few minutes. Saint Jude stands in a dark nook at one corner of the building. He's the patron saint of lost causes. Which is kind of perfect, since sometimes surviving middle school feels like a lost cause.

Here comes Maya. I lift my hand to wave, but she walks right by. I guess she didn't see me. "Hey, Maya," I yell. A bunch of kids turn around and look at me, but not Maya. I go after her as fast as I can. Something's wrong. I know she heard me.

I catch up to her in front of our geometry classroom. "Maya? Hey, Maya, what's wrong?" I have to grab her arm to make her turn around. When she does, I see her dark brown eyes are too shiny, and her jaw is clenched. She shakes my hand off.

"What's wrong?" I ask again. "Why didn't you answer me?"

"I'm supposed to be the smartest one. Me." Maya takes a shaky breath and blows her bangs out of her eyes. "And now *you're* some kind of genius? And that's all anyone wants to talk about. *You're* the smartest kid in school? *You?* What does that make me? Second best?"

"But it doesn't mean anything. It's just what some stupid test says." I don't know why she's so upset. And I don't know what to say to make it better.

"Maybe it doesn't mean anything to you. But it means everything to me." And my second-best friend, the one person I thought could help me figure this genius thing out, walks into class without me.

Three

When I got to school today, I hoped something would have taken my place on the St. Jude gossip hotline. That somehow everyone would have forgotten about me, and things would be back to normal. That Maya would be back to normal.

No such luck. Stares? Yep. Whispers? Yep. Number of times I've been called Einstein? Six—make that seven. Second-best friend—still not talking to me.

And first best friend not where he's supposed to be.

"Hey, where're you going?" I ask.

"The Clubhouse—same as you." Linc's voice is flat, and his smile is missing.

"She found out." It's not a question.

"She found out," says Linc. "Yesterday. She was on the phone all night with Mr. Dooley and Mrs. Capistrano." Mrs. Capistrano is our guidance counselor. Linc spends a lot of time with her trying to "find the key to unlocking his love for learning."

"When I got to homeroom, there was a schedule change form on my desk," says Linc.

"Wow, your mom's good," I say.

"Yeah." Not a good yeah.

"So, are you ready for this?"

"For what? This class? Sure, I guess." Linc scratches his head. "Hey, do you know who else is in it? Any cute girls?"

Now Linc's smile is back. I roll my eyes at him. Ever since he found his first armpit hair, girls are all Linc thinks about. Or talks about.

"Here it is." I stop walking. And rolling.

The Clubhouse is a small room next to the science lab where a lot of after-school clubs meet. And it's the home of our new enrichment class.

When we walk in, there's a note on the whiteboard. It reads, "Sit anywhere you'd like. We'll start getting to know each other in a few minutes."

Terrific.

I forget about the teacher while I analyze the best place to sit. When a teacher lets us pick, I always choose a seat

14

in the middle. Up front gets you too much attention, and some teachers purposely pick on the kids in the back row. The middle is safe. But there's no middle here.

The desks are arranged in a half-moon so everyone will be in the front row. And there are only six of them. Like I knew she would be, Maya is in one of the six. She flicks her eyes up at me for just a second and then looks back down like she doesn't know me. Okay.

Before I can take another step, my backpack goes flying and sends me into the wall with it. I look and see that someone who looks like a full-grown man just tripped over it. It's Ty Easterbrook, eighth grader and star of the St. Jude basketball team. Great. He probably sprained his ankle and now the season will be ruined. And it'll be my fault.

"Sorry. Are you okay?" I ask. My shoulder stings from where it hit the corner of the wall.

"It's all right. Hey, nice backpack." Ty socks me in the arm. I think it's supposed to be friendly, but he knocks me into the wall again. Now my shoulder really hurts.

Linc waves me over to where he's set up base. I slide into the seat next to him, the one closest to the window. And the one farthest away from Maya and the empty seat next to her. The seat I would be sitting in if we were still friends.

"What are you doing tripping Ty Easterbrook? And did you see he has a mustache? How can I compete with that? A mustache? The girls won't even notice me." Linc's voice cracks every time he asks a question. "Did you know there were going to be eighth graders in here?"

"No, I didn't know. And I didn't trip him; he fell over my backpack. And it's not a mustache. It's just a few hairs above his lip."

"It's a mustache. Great, he looks like a man and then there's us." Linc has a point. Some of the guys at St. Jude look like they're already done with puberty. We don't.

Linc slaps a wrinkled folder down on his desk and searches around under his hair until he pulls a pen out from behind his ear. A pen with a chewed on top that he probably found at the bottom of his locker. I guess he's ready.

I unzip my backpack and grab a fresh notebook and the lucky Superman pen my grandpa gave me. Just holding it in my hand makes me feel less anxious. I hope it's enough to keep my nervous stomach from kicking in. Bad things happen when my nervous stomach kicks in.

"Okay, everyone. Let's get started."

I turn and look at the person standing in the front of the room. Our teacher? Really? She turns and writes her name on the board. "Sister Stephanie."

Linc stretches his leg sideways and kicks me in the shin. I shrug.

"Sister Stephanie?" It's Maya. "*You're* a nun?"

Her question isn't quite as rude as it sounds. I mean, we go to a Catholic school. We've seen nuns before—lots of times. We've had nuns for teachers. But not like this.

"Yep. I'm Sister Stephanie. But everyone calls me Sister Stevie. You can, too."

Sister Stephanie, or I guess Stevie, is wearing a long-sleeved white dress that goes from her neck down to just above the floor and a black veil on her head. She doesn't look much older than any of us. Maybe it's the curly hair that looks like it was colored with a yellow crayon, maybe it's the dimples when she smiles. Or just maybe it's the neon pink Converse peeking out from below her dress. She smiles at all of us and blows a piece of hair out of her face. This is our teacher.

Sister Stevie grabs a huge blue ball like the one my mom uses to exercise and sits on it so she's facing us. She has a remote control in her hand and, when she clicks a button, some kind of classical music starts playing. So far, so weird.

"Now, let's get to know each other." Sister Stevie's smile is big. It makes her look too cheerful to be a teacher.

I peek around the room and see everyone else staring

at Sister Stevie. I don't know what we were expecting from this class, but she wasn't it.

"So, first on my list is Gabriel Carpenter," says Sister Stevie. "Gabriel. Like the angel?"

I hear a snicker and some guy with more freckles than I've ever seen says, "Isn't that sweet. But where's your halo?"

"It's Gabe," I say quickly. "Just call me Gabe." And yes, it's Gabriel like the angel. Every teacher I've ever had always asks the same question like they're the first person to think of it.

"Gabe it is then," says Sister Stevie. "And you know, archangels, like Gabriel, are fierce and powerful warriors." Hmmm, maybe this will be okay after all.

"A warrior? Hah. That's almost as funny as Gabe being a genius," says Maya. So, I guess she's still mad at me about the whole genius thing. She acts like it's my fault. And now the only girl in school I could talk to won't talk to me.

Sister Stevie looks at Maya and then at me. She scribbles some kind of note and then moves on to the next name on her list, Ty Easterbrook. The guy with the freckles is Cameron Goodrich, and then there's Maya and Linc.

Finally, Sister Stevie gets to the last name on the list and the reason Linc hasn't been able to close his mouth or blink since class started. Rachel Zimmerman. Eighth grader. The prettiest girl at St. Jude and Linc's ultimate crush. The chances of Linc learning anything in this class just went way down.

"Each of you was selected to be part of this class for a reason," says Sister Stevie. "This is such a special opportunity. I hope you're all as excited to be here as I am."

I'm not. I don't think anyone could be that excited.

"You said we were going to get to know *each other*," says Maya.

"Yes."

"But you didn't tell us anything about you."

"What would you like to know?" Sister Stevie is still smiling even though Maya's chin is jutting out, and her arms are crossed tightly in front of her.

"Two main things, to start." Maya is in full interrogation mode. I've been on the wrong side of her interrogations. My pits start to sweat in sympathy for Sister. "First, what are your qualifications? And second, is this going to be a religion class? Because I didn't think it was going to be a religion class."

"Those are both fair questions, Maya. Thank you for asking." Sister Stevie shifts around on the giant blue ball and straightens her veil again. It doesn't seem to want to stay on her head.

"One of my fellow sisters used to teach here—she's retired now but is still great friends with Mrs. Capistrano. She told me about this class, and I offered to teach it. As for my qualifications, I have three degrees including masters' in both physics and theology, and I'm finishing up my master's in education. I'll teach at the university level eventually. But I'm thrilled to be here now."

Wow. I'm not entirely sure what all of that means, but what it sounds like is that Sister Stevie knows a lot about a lot.

"Second question. Is this a religion class? Would it be a bad thing if it were?" Sister Stevie looks from one to the other of us. Nobody says anything. "Gabe? What do you think?"

She wants to know what I think. I can't tell her what I really think. I can't tell a nun that I kind of feel like we've got the religion thing covered in actual religion class every day, so I make a weird shrug, nod, head-shaking motion that could mean anything.

"No, this isn't going to be a religion class. But, it isn't *not* going to be a religion class, either. We're going to focus mainly in two areas: science and literature," says Sister Stevie. "But we'll also talk about the contributions to these and other areas by religious people."

Sister Stevie pushes a button on the remote, and the

music gets louder. "For instance, does anyone know who the composer of this piece is?"

"Vivaldi," says Maya.

"That's correct. It is Vivaldi's *Four Seasons*. Vivaldi was a priest. And has anyone heard of Gregor Mendel?" Of course we have. All six hands go up—even Linc's. We learned about him in fourth-grade science and again last year. "He was a monk."

Sister Stevie keeps talking. She talks for so long that I look out the window and forget to listen for a minute. The view is mostly just the reddish-brown brick wall of the building next door. But I discover that if I crane my neck just right, I can see clouds whipping across the sky. These are cumulonimbus clouds, which means today we'll have rain and maybe even a storm. Cumulonimbus clouds can have as much as 150 thousand tons of water in them. But if these move fast enough and it doesn't rain too much, maybe Linc and I can still shoot baskets after school.

"I don't understand. What do you mean no grades?" Maya's voice gets higher and louder at the end of her question. It's the higher and louder that pull me back from thinking about clouds.

I must have stopped listening for too long because I have no idea what she's talking about. No grades?

"That's right, Maya," says Sister Stevie. "There will be no letter grades in this class. Our goal is to teach you how to expand your minds, not to worry about getting yet another A." Sister Stevie smiles—again with the dimples. Maya doesn't smile back. At all.

"But how will we know who's the best?" Maya asks. "How will we know who's really the smartest?" She turns in her seat and glares at me, blowing her bangs up out of her eyes. I pretend not to notice the look, but even after I turn away, I can still feel it. It's like a prickling on the back of my neck. We used to be friends.

Sister Stevie talks some more about how grades don't measure everything and how we're not "gifted" but rather we're all "gifts." I don't get what that means and really, I don't know what to think about any of this. I mean we've always gotten grades. My parents might flip out. Linc's will for sure. And it looks like any minute now Maya's head is going to explode.

Four

I close my eyes and imagine myself making this shot. Woomp, woomp, woomp. Stop, aim, and shoot. Clang. Off the rim. And I missed. Again.

"That's P." Linc gets the rebound.

"Which one?" I ask.

"Third." He stands over next to my mom's rosebushes, dribbles twice, and shoots. Swish. He looks at me, shrugs, and goes to get the ball.

It stopped raining during the walk home from school. But, thanks to layers of stratocumulus clouds, there's no sun and, since it's November, it's kind of cold. But North Carolina cold, so an extra sweatshirt means it's still a good day for basketball.

I kick at the jagged crack at the spot where the driveway bends toward the garage on the side of our house. "So what do you think about no grades from Sister Stevie?"

"I think it's great. You know I don't belong in that class with you brains. This way not everybody has to know." Linc bounces the ball to me. "But I'm not telling my parents until I have to."

Woomp, woomp, woomp. Stop, aim, and shoot. Silence. That's the sound of my shot missing the net, the rim, and the backboard. Then, plop, crunch. That's the sound of the ball landing in a puddle and then in my mom's flowers. Pansies, I think. I don't know why she keeps planting flowers behind the hoop. They always end up flat or dead. And she always plants more.

"That's O," says Linc. "The second one."

Linc and I play basketball at my house most days after school. His parents both work late, and he doesn't have any brothers or sisters, so if he didn't come here, he'd be home by himself all the time. Instead, he rides his bike over, and we play H-I-P-P-O-P-O-T-A-M-U-S. We used to play H-O-R-S-E, but the games only took about five minutes. I still never win, but at least it takes longer for me to lose.

"What do you mean you don't belong in the class?" I

say. "You're smart." It's true. Linc is smart, at least about stuff he cares about.

"Not that kind of smart. Not like you. It's like your brain has its own way of doing things." Linc goes over to where we drew a foul line with chalk and, without even dribbling, throws the ball up. It circles the rim a couple of times and then drops in. "Like, what's your favorite number?"

"You know it's 15. Why?" And I miss another shot. "I know, that's T."

"Why is 15 your favorite number?"

"I've told you. It's because if you take the numeric position in the alphabet of the letters in my name and add them up, you get 15. Like G is the seventh number so it's 7, A is 1, B is 2, and E is 5. So 7+1+2+5 is 15. And that's my lucky number."

"See, no one else's brain works like that," says Linc. And he makes a shot from at least three-point range. I know before I take the shot that it's going to be A. At least it's almost over. Just M, U, and S to go.

"Maybe, but that doesn't help me stink at basketball any less," I say. "So how did you pick a favorite number?"

"I picked 13 because everyone else thinks it's unlucky, so I figure maybe it'll be lucky for me." Linc spins the basketball on his finger, turns around, and throws it over his shoulder toward the net. Finally, he misses a shot. "But there is one thing I do want to learn in that class."

"What?" I take an easy layup and actually make it.

I pass the ball to Linc who grins and says, "How to make Rachel Zimmerman fall for me." He makes his layup and tosses the ball in my direction.

"Do you think about anything besides girls anymore?" I ask. "And seriously, why would Rachel fall for you?" Maybe it's because I'm laughing that I totally miss the ball when Linc throws it. But when I turn around to go get it, there she is. Becca Piccarelli. And instead of running to get the basketball, I slip in a puddle of water, and I'm the one who falls.

Five

"Are you hurt?" Becca's voice sounds like she's trying not to laugh, but I don't really know because I can't look at her. Seriously, I cannot pick my head up and look at her.

"Hey, Becca," says Linc. He reaches down, grabs the back of my sweatshirt and pulls up until I'm on my feet again instead of my butt. "Don't worry, he'll be fine."

I make a noise that sounds like, "Uunnggh," and shuffle over to where the basketball came to rest against the front tire of Linc's bike. I pick it up, hold it in my hands, and remind myself to breathe. I tell myself this is no big deal, and I can handle it. This is a lie.

I turn around and see Linc talking and laughing with Becca like it's nothing. Like she's just anybody. Like he doesn't notice how her shiny brown ponytail bounces when she walks, and that it curves almost like a question mark down to a spot right between her shoulder blades. Like he doesn't notice how she smells like vanilla and rain. Like he doesn't notice that her nose crinkles up when she smiles. But I do. I notice all of it.

"What'd you do now, Gabe, pee your pants?" It's Sabrina. She's standing on the front porch, arms folded across her middle and a smirk on her face.

"What are you talking about?" Then I notice that my butt feels cold. And wet. Oh great, when I fell in the puddle, my pants got soaked.

"No, I didn't. I fell in a puddle, okay."

"Oh, like that's better. Come on, Becca, you don't want to talk to them," Sabrina says. "I got my toe shoes today. I want to show you how I can go *en pointe*." Sabrina tries to sound French whenever she talks about ballet. It just makes her sound stupid.

"Dancing on your toes is going to give you claw feet." I make claws out of my hands and take a step toward her like I'm going to come after her with my claws. She jumps back.

A giggle spurts out of Becca. Sabrina glares at her and then at me. "Shut up, Gabe." She drags Becca inside by the hand and slams the door.

Becca Piccarelli is Sabrina's best friend. She lives exactly thirteen houses down on the other side of the street. And since Becca has been my sister's best friend since preschool, she has been to my house approximately 17,000 times. I used to think she was annoying. I mean, Sabrina is. And Becca probably was, too. But then something changed. Well, everything changed.

It was last summer. Sabrina had been moping around for four long weeks because Becca was away at some horse camp in Kentucky. Every day we had to listen to Sabrina moan about how there was "nothing to do," and she was going to "die of boredom."

Finally, one Monday afternoon, the doorbell rang and, since I was the closest, I opened the door. And there she was. Becca. Only something happened while she was gone, and she didn't look like Becca anymore. Her hair was different, and she had new freckles, and she seemed taller and somehow softer. And I stood there with my mouth open and couldn't speak. I haven't been able to say anything that's not stupid to her since. My strategy now is to hide in my room whenever she comes over.

"Well, that was smooth," says Linc. "I'm pretty sure if you ever want her to like you, you're going to have to talk to her."

"I know. But I can't. My brain stops working whenever

I see her. It's a total blank. And when I open my mouth, nothing comes out."

"Your brain stops working? But you're supposed to be a genius," says Linc. "What good is being a genius if you can't talk to girls?"

I don't answer. I just take the ball and throw up another shot. "And that's S," I say. Even though it's not. "Game over."

I can hear my mom coming from the other end of the house. My mom is small—even I'm almost as tall as she is—but somehow she sounds like a large elephant when she walks. It's probably because she's always on a mission.

I slide the three-foot-long LEGO-set suspension bridge I was working on—it's not playing, it's engineering—under my bed and grab my math book. An open notebook, my lucky math pencil, and a concentrating wrinkle between my eyebrows, and it looks like I've been doing homework for hours.

The pounding steps stop right outside my door. There's a weird pause and then my mom knocks. Softly. It's the pause and the softly that make my radar go up.

"Come in."

The door opens and there's my mom. She smiles down at me and then looks around the room. My bed—where I'm leaning—isn't neatly made. I just threw my blue and green striped comforter over my sheets this morning. Tiny frown.

My sock drawer is open a crack, and one white sock is sticking out. Bigger frown, but she doesn't say anything. She closes her eyes for a second and, when she reopens them, the smile is back. Yep, something's up.

She straightens her apron—my mom runs a cookie catering business called Heavenly Bites—and says, "Honey, I saw Mrs. Piccarelli at church this morning. She asked if you'd do her a favor," says my mom.

"A favor? What kind of favor?"

"Well, tutoring actually. Becca is having a lot of trouble with math, and I told her I was sure you could help."

"No." It feels like I can't get the word out fast enough. "I can't. I mean—just, no." Tutor Becca? How can I tutor Becca when I can't talk to her? Or even look at her. My stomach clenches and my ears burn.

"What? Why can't you?" My mom is looking at me like I have a third eye or a booger hanging out of my nose.

There's no way I can tell her the real reason. So I say, "Because she's Sabrina's annoying friend. And they make fun of me all the time. And because—well—I just don't want to."

"Honey, Mrs. Piccarelli asked me, and I already said yes. I know I probably should have talked to you about it first, but I really didn't think you'd mind." The stomach clenching gets worse, and now my face is as hot as my ears. My entire head is in danger of bursting into flames.

Okay, so I'm going to have to sit across a table from Becca and try to talk to her about math. When I can't talk to her about anything. But since I can't tell my mom the truth, and I can't think of anything else to say to convince her this is a bad idea, I just sigh and lay my head back on my bed.

"Fine. I guess I'll do it."

My mom smiles and reaches down to try to fix my hair. My unfixable hair. "Thanks honey, I really appreciate this, and I know Mrs. Piccarelli will, too."

Then, just as my mom goes to leave, the thing happens that always happens when the clenching in my stomach gets this bad. It doesn't make a sound. It doesn't have to.

My mom stops in the doorway, turns around, sniffs the air and says, "Gabe?"

"Sorry," I mumble. Whenever I get really nervous about something, my stomach feels like someone's squeezing it in his fist. And when it gets squeezed, well, bad things happen. Bad smelling things happen.

I start scribbling in my notebook like I'm getting back to my homework. Then I think of something important that my mom didn't tell me. "Hey, Mom, when am I supposed to start tutoring Becca?"

"Tomorrow after school." She blows me a kiss and closes the door behind her.

I groan and let my head fall back against my bed. Eyes pointing up, I start to say a prayer asking for help. I'm not sure who to direct this prayer to. I mean, even though it's a huge problem to me, it seems like God probably has bigger stuff to worry about. Mary's not the right answer—it'd feel like talking to my mom, which I'm not going to do. Is there a patron saint of talking to girls? Hmmm . . . might be worth researching. For now I just send a quick one up to Saint Jude.

I stand up, pace from one end of my long, narrow room to the other and then flop face down on my bed and groan. Then I groan again, louder this time. I turn my head to the left to see if the guys noticed. It doesn't look like they did.

The guys are Celsius and Fahrenheit, my goldfish. They were my consolation prize when the dog I got for my eighth birthday had to go back after it turned out

Sabrina is allergic. She was all red-nosed and sneezing, and there was even a rash. I was mad about it for a long time. But now I like having the guys. They're easy to talk to.

"What am I going to do?" I ask. Celsius flips his black tail and swims in the other direction, and Fahrenheit glugs. They don't know either.

Six

More stares, more whispers, more not being able to open my locker. Oh, and the squeak in my backpack wheel is back. So far, today totally stinks. When I get to The Clubhouse, I clomp (me) and squeak (my backpack) across the room and collapse into my chair. I slide down until my butt is barely on the seat and stare out the window. A bad mood settles around me like a cloud. A cumulonimbus cloud.

"What's wrong?" says Linc as he flops into his seat. "Did somebody take your lunch money?" He laughs at his own joke.

"Not funny," I say. "Today's just a rotten day, okay?"

"It's a beautiful day in here." Even if I wasn't watching

Linc, I would know where he was looking and what, or who, he was talking about. He's staring at Rachel Zimmerman like she's a pizza with pepperoni, sausage, and extra cheese. Linc loves pizza with pepperoni, sausage, and extra cheese.

"You might want to at least try to play it cool," I whisper. "There are only six of us in here. She can see you staring at her."

"She can hear y'all, too," drawls Rachel. She looks over at us, gives a tiny smile, and goes back to playing with the gold cross she wears around her neck and reading a book of what looks like poetry. Linc swoons like a girl. I laugh a little. I can't help it.

Sister Stevie turns on the classical music, grabs the big blue ball from the corner of the room, and sits on it. And class begins.

"So I told you this class is going to be different," says Sister Stevie. "But it's more than just special projects, self-directed study, and no letter grades."

Those are a lot of differences. What else is there? Is she going to make everybody sit on exercise balls?

"Principal Dooley and I have a vision for this program. We want it to be special. So, we've decided that this class will compete in the Middle School Academic Olympics. We'll be up against middle schools from all over

North Carolina. Isn't that exciting?" Sister Stevie bounces up and down on her ball like a little kid. Any minute now she's going to fall off.

"Exciting?" says Ty. "I'm on the basketball team, you know. I don't have time for stuff like that." Ty shifts in his seat and tugs on the edge of the jersey he's wearing over a green golf shirt and khaki pants—our school uniform. On game days all the players and the cheerleaders wear their jerseys. That way we're all sure to know who's a star and who's not.

"Yes, Ty, I know everyone's busy. But this is an extraordinary opportunity for all of you. And it's going to be so much fun," says Sister Stevie. She smiles at us as hard as she can, but nobody smiles back.

"So what's it all about?" asks Linc. "What's so fun about it, and what do we have to do?" I know what he's thinking. This sounds like extra work, and Linc doesn't do extra work.

"Well, a lot of that's up to you. The most exciting part is that although you'll each have an individual entry, we'll compete as a team. So working together is going to be essential," says Sister Stevie. "You'll decide on an overall theme and then each of you will come up with your own project that explores that theme. For example, if we picked the human body, everyone could pick an organ system and go from there."

That might be all right. I'd pick the integumentary system—all of a person's skin, hair, and nails. It's awesome how its job is to protect the body, kind of like a warrior.

"Okay, so what's our theme?" asks Maya. She has her notebook out and her pen at the ready. Maya always writes down instructions and follows them exactly.

"That's up to all of you," says Sister Stevie. She sparkles at Maya like this is a good answer. Maya huffs and strums her fingers on her desk.

"You might want to pick a team captain to help you get started," says Sister Stevie.

"I'll be the captain." Maya turns and glares at each of us, ending with me, daring anybody to tell her no.

"All right." Rachel has her poetry book tucked under her notebook and is still trying to read it. Nobody else says anything.

"Okay, Maya's our captain," says Sister Stevie. "I have a folder for each of you that explains the competition and gives you some idea starters." She gives each of us a thick folder.

"Take these home and read them over and then come back on Monday ready to brainstorm. The competition is only two months away."

Sister Stevie keeps talking, but I stop listening to her because I'm busy listening to the weird humming noise coming from Linc. He's gazing at Rachel again. I stretch my leg out and kick him in the shin. He turns and grins at me like a crazy person.

Why is he smiling like that? I don't ask because I don't want to know.

"Wait, you forgot something," says Cameron.

"What's that?" asks Sister Stevie.

"We need a team name," he says. "And I have the perfect one."

Cameron pauses and looks around like he's making sure we're all listening. "G.A.S. Attack."

What?

"Because this class is called Greater Achieving Students, right?" says Cameron.

Sister Stevie nods and raises her eyebrows at him.

"Everyone thinks we're nerds for being in here. But if we're funny about it, we'll show them that we're not."

"Nobody thinks I'm a nerd, Cameron," says Ty. He jabs at his folder with a pen.

"Sure they do, they think we're all nerds," says Cameron. "So let's go with that. Our team name can be 'G.A.S. Attack.' You know, gas?" He makes a farting noise with his mouth and cracks up. Rachel giggles a little and rolls her eyes. Linc guffaws. I don't laugh even a little. There's nothing funny about gas.

"This isn't a joke," says Maya. "Why do you want to make us a joke?" She says something under her breath in Spanish. It's not something nice. Maya's mom is from Mexico, and her dad is from China so she knows a lot of creative ways to insult someone in both Spanish and Mandarin. And since we were friends until two days ago, I know them too. This one was Spanish, and it was a good one.

I can't help it, I laugh. And I think Maya almost smiles at me before she puffs at her bangs and whips her head back around. Yep, still mad.

Linc is sitting at our usual table in the cafeteria—Maya isn't. I can see Linc, but I can't get to him. A sea of bodies surrounds me and the sound of hundreds of kids all talking at once seems to suck the air out of the room.

I fight my way through, trying not to notice that today's "special," an open-faced hot turkey sandwich with gravy, has a weird smell that's not at all turkey-like.

"Hey, you made it," says Linc. He's almost done eating his bag lunch.

"Yeah. Hey, does this turkey smell funny to you?" I try to wave it in front of his face, but he deflects and leans way back.

"You know I don't eat the food here. I don't want to smell it either. But yeah, something's not right. It looks sort of gray." Linc laughs and takes an enormous bite out of his apple. He keeps talking anyway. "So what's the plan for this afternoon? Hoops in your driveway?"

"Uh no, not today. I've got a thing." I haven't told Linc about tutoring Becca. I'm not sure why.

"What kind of thing?" Linc takes another bite of his apple, this one even bigger. It's kind of impressive. Or disgusting.

I look down at my lunch, both interested and disgusted to observe that the gravy has turned into something more solid than liquid. "I have to tutor Becca after school. In math."

Linc starts to laugh, and then he starts to choke. After a few coughs and a thump on the back from me, he's okay. But he's still laughing.

"Wait, did you say you're tutoring Becca? Where?"

"Her house. And what's so funny anyway?" I ask. "Didn't you hear the news? I'm supposed to be pretty smart. Like a genius even." I cross my eyes at Linc.

"What's so funny is picturing you trying to tutor her when you can't even talk to her. How's that gonna work?" says Linc.

Of course this is what I've been worried about since my mom first sprang this plan on me.

"Shut up," I say. I take my fork and stab a piece of turkey. The gravy sticks to it like it's made out of glue. I put the bite in my mouth and chew. And chew. And chew some more. It's not working. I don't know what this is, but it's not turkey.

Linc clears his throat and kicks me under the table.

"What?" I say.

He opens his eyes extra wide and, looking over my head, says, "Hey, Becca, how's it going?"

Becca? I look over my shoulder and there she is, standing right behind me.

"Hey, Linc. Hi, Gabe." She smiles and her nose crinkles and my mind goes blank. Just blank.

I try to say something. I really do. But then I remember that I still have this unchewable wad of turkey in my mouth, so I just nod and kind of grunt.

"So, Gabe, my mom said you're coming over after school to help me with math. Is that still okay?" says Becca.

I nod again and try not to look as stupid as I feel.

She looks at me like she's waiting for something until I guess she figures out I'm not going to say anything. "Well, okay. I guess I'll see you then." Becca waggles her fingers at us and goes back to the table where she was sitting with Sabrina and their other friends.

I turn back around and look at Linc. He just shakes his head.

"I know, I know," I say. "It's bad. What am I going to do?"

"I don't know," says Linc. "But you'd better come up with a plan fast. Because what you just did? You can't do that."

Seven

I scuff the toe of my shoe back and forth along the edge of the welcome mat on Becca's porch and try to come up with a reason not to ring the doorbell. Do I feel sick? No, not unless you count the clenching in my stomach. And I don't want to think about that. Do I hear my mom calling me home to help with an emergency? Nope. Is there a storm coming? I squint up at the sky. Not one cloud.

Okay, this is it. Breathe in, breathe out. I reach my finger out to press the button, but before I can, the door pops open and there she is. Becca.

"Hey, Gabe, I saw you walk up a few minutes ago. What were you doing?"

"Uh, nothing." Great. Off to a good start.

She looks at me and tilts her head to the side like she's trying to figure out what's going on. Then she smiles. "Well, come on in."

"Okay." So I'm not going to impress her with my conversation. Let's hope I remember how to do math.

"Gabe, honey, hi. Come on in," says Mrs. Piccarelli. "I thought you and Becca could study in the dining room. No one will bother you in there."

There are five Piccarelli kids—Becca's the oldest and the only girl—so it's always loud and crazy at their house. But right now it's quiet, which makes me think Mrs. Piccarelli must have the boys tied up in the basement.

Becca and I sit down. I breathe in and try to calm down. I tell myself this is no big deal. It's just math. Then I look at Becca and it happens again—my brain turns off.

"Okay, here's what we've been working on," says Becca.

She turns her textbook so that we can both see it, if we lean in close. I do and get a noseful of her shampoo—it's green apple today. Becca fiddles with her pencil and flips a few pages back and forth. "It's multiplying and dividing fractions. I got so confused and then I got a D+ on the test and well, I just don't get it."

Becca twists her ponytail around and around her finger

and, when I sneak a look at her, her cheeks are pink, and she's staring down at the table.

"You don't get it *yet*," I say. She looks at me with her lower lip between her teeth and a tiny wrinkle between her eyebrows. I look down at the book. All those numbers make me feel calmer. "Let's see what you had trouble with on the test."

Becca hands me the test. I take it, making sure not to touch her hand. While I look at the test, Becca fidgets. She shifts in her chair, twirls her hair some more, flips pages in her notebook, and sighs a sigh that sounds like it comes from her toes.

"It's not so bad," I say. "Really. We can fix this."

"Really? Because my dad tried to help me and . . ."

"Not so helpful?"

She giggles. "Not so helpful. It's just that—well, he's an engineer. He does math stuff all day long. He's disappointed that I'm not good at it."

"Yeah, mine is disappointed that I'm not good at sports. I guess it's a dad thing. Wanting you to be something you're not."

Why did I say that? I didn't mean to say anything like that. When I look up, Becca is looking right at me. But it's a different kind of looking—like she really sees me. I make myself look back at her.

A clump of slimy green goo flies over my head and plops onto the red D+ on Becca's test. Kissing noises and snickering come from behind me.

"Matthew! Peter! Get out," yells Becca. Two of the brothers must have escaped. "Mo—om!"

Mrs. Piccarelli pops her head in from the kitchen. "What happened?" She sees the goo and hears the snickering and smooching sounds. "Boys, get back to the basement now or no TV tonight."

There's the sound of feet pounding on the floor then a door opens and almost immediately slams shut hard enough to knock the crucifix on the wall crooked. Mrs. Piccarelli straightens it, then plucks the goo off the table, and goes back to the kitchen. "They won't bother you anymore," she says over her shoulder.

Whatever I was going to say before Becca's little brothers showed up is gone. I take her math book and a fresh piece of paper and start explaining. And something weird happens. As long as I'm talking about math, and as long as I don't look right at her, I can talk to Becca without tripping over my words or sounding stupid.

I give Becca a few problems to work through on her own and tell myself not to stare at her while she does them. The way she talks to herself under her breath and taps her pencil on the tip of her nose while she's thinking make it impossible. She hands me the paper when she's finished so I can check her work.

I look up and grin. "You got them right. All of them."

"Really?" Becca's face brightens. "Wow. I guess it was the way you explained it. All of a sudden it just made sense." She looks at me and smiles. And her nose crinkles up. And there it goes again. My brain. Blank.

"I guess you really are a genius," says Becca. I look down at the table and shrug.

"What does being a genius feel like anyway?"

"It doesn't feel like anything." I rub the dimple in my chin and keep looking down. "That's not true. Kids at school stare at me and talk about me, my parents say my grades need to be even better, and some people are mad at me."

"Like Sabrina?"

"She's always mad at me about something. But no, it's Maya."

"Why would Maya be mad at you?" Becca's forehead goes wrinkly again, but then smoothes right back out. "Oh, because she's always been the smartest."

"Yeah. And she doesn't get that she still is the smartest. It's just a stupid test." I start rolling my lucky math pencil back and forth on the table. "And now she doesn't want to be my friend anymore."

"You just need to talk to her. I'm sure she doesn't mean it." There it is again. She's looking at me like I'm not just Sabrina's brother. Like I'm me. And I know what I have to do. Leave.

"Okay, so I'm gonna go." I stand up so fast I almost topple over my chair. I grab the handle of my backpack and head for the front door.

"Um, okay. Well, thanks for helping me." Becca half-trots down the hall to catch up with me. "I guess my mom said we're supposed to do this every week, right?"

I nod. I can't look at her. My stomach clenches so hard I almost can't stand up straight. I know what's going to happen. I have to get out. Now.

"Well, bye," says Becca.

She closes the door behind me, and I lean back on it for a minute. When I let out the breath I've been holding, something else comes out, too. But I made it.

As I walk down the street toward my house, my smile is so big it's making my cheeks hurt. It wasn't perfect. But I talked to Becca a little bit. And there was a minute when it felt like she was talking to me, Gabe, not just Sabrina's brother. Best of all, I'm coming back next week.

Linc is sitting on my front porch. I see him before he

sees me. He's dribbling a basketball between his feet, head hanging down.

"Hey, what are you doing here?" I say.

Linc's head snaps up and, after a second or two, he gives it a quick shake and jumps to his feet. "Waiting for you. How'd it go? Did you actually talk to Becca? How's your stomach? You didn't fart, did you?" Linc bounces on his feet and twirls the basketball on his finger. Linc thinks farts are hilarious, but he knows for me, it's no joke.

"Not even a genius can keep up with all of your questions." I laugh. "No, I didn't fart. Had a close call, but I made it out the door in time. And yes, I talked to her." The cheek-hurting smile starts all over again.

"You did? Really? Just about math? Tell me."

"I'm trying to tell you. But you have to stop talking first." I grab the basketball from Linc. I try to spin it on my finger like he did, which doesn't work—at all. The ball ends up in the middle of the front yard.

"Okay, we mostly talked about math, but we talked about other stuff, too." Linc rolls his eyes at me, and, with his lips shut tight, motions with his hand for me to go on.

I open my mouth to tell him about Becca talking to me and looking at me like I'm someone more than just her best friend's brother. But I kind of don't want to say it out loud. So I just park my backpack, go get the ball and yell over my shoulder, "Come on, let's play some H-I-P-P-O-P-O-T-A-M-U-S. I feel lucky today."

"Okay, let's see what you've got." Linc runs over to the basketball hoop, grabs the piece of chalk that we keep next to the base, measures off six big steps, and draws our free throw line. I walk over, stand on the line, and dribble the ball a couple times to warm up.

Like I always do, I close my eyes and try to see myself making the shot. Woomp, woomp, woomp. Stop, aim, and shoot. But this time, there's no clang. This time, there's a swish. An actual swish. My mouth drops open and then I smile. I smile so hard I think I pull a muscle in my face.

"Whoa, you are feeling lucky today," says Linc. "Nice shot. Let's see what I can do with it." He steps to where I'm standing, gives me a little shove out of the way, laughs, and shoots. He misses.

Linc frowns at the basket, and then he looks at me. "That's H,' he says. "That's H on me. You're in the lead."

In the hundreds of games we've played, I've only been in the lead one other time. And that day, Linc was coming down with the flu.

We look at each other and laugh. "Your shot," says Linc.

I want to see if this was a fluke or maybe I'm finally getting better. So I walk to the spot on the chalk line where I can see my shoeprint. I put my shoe exactly on top of it. And again I close my eyes and see the shot in my mind. I open my eyes, dribble three times, and shoot. And there it is—swish. Again. I made another shot.

"I don't believe it," says Linc.

I don't either, which is why I don't move from the spot.

"I've never made two in a row," I say. "Never."

"Okay, my turn." This time Linc takes his time and makes the shot.

Linc gets the ball and looks at me, his eyebrows raised up so high they disappear under his hair. "One tutoring session with Becca Piccarelli and now you can shoot? Spill it—what happened?"

Before I can answer, the side door pops opens. My mom sticks her head out and says, "Supper's at 5:30. Do you want to stay, Linc?"

"Sure, thanks. My parents aren't going to be home until later," says Linc.

Supper is at 5:30 at my house every night. My dad is a physical therapist, and his last appointment ends at 4:30 every day. He's home by 5:15, and supper is ready fifteen minutes later. What my mom makes for supper changes, but everything else is exactly the same.

I check my watch—I wear it on my right wrist because I'm left-handed—to see how much time we have left. I usually have to push up the sleeve of my jacket to see my watch. But not today.

Oh, no! Has it finally happened? I check my left wrist. It doesn't look like it's sticking out as much. Has using only my right arm to pull my backpack with all of my books in it done this to me? Is my right arm longer than my left? Am I deformed?

"Linc, do my arms look uneven to you?" I hold them out in front of me.

Linc is trying to line up a shot. "What are you talking about?"

"This is serious. Does my right arm look longer than my left arm?" This time I put them down at my sides, holding them perfectly straight.

Linc makes his shot and turns to look at me. He asks again, "What are you talking about?"

"Okay, you know how I can only pull my backpack with my right arm?" Linc frowns at me. "Well, I can—right arm only. And you know I can never open my stupid locker so I always have all of my books in my pack. Which means it's really heavy."

Linc starts to laugh. "Wait, are you telling me that you

think your right arm has stretched from dragging your backpack around?" He looks up at the sky and guffaws.

"It's not funny," I say. "I'm going to find out. You can come with me or stay out here and do your comedian thing."

I walk through the house and straight to my room. The measuring tape I snuck out of my mom's sewing kit is in the back of my underwear drawer. I'm using my chin to hold one end of the measuring tape at the top of my left shoulder when Linc catches up with me.

"You're serious about this," he says.

I don't answer him. I finish measuring and mumble, "Left arm, 24 inches exactly." Then I measure my right arm. Twice. "24 and $1/8$ inches. It's $1/8$ of an inch longer! It actually happened, my arm grew longer." I look up at Linc. "I've been worried this was going to happen and now it has. I'm a freak."

Linc's talking but I can't hear him over the buzzing in my head. Is this only the beginning? Will my right arm keep getting longer? If this keeps up, eventually my arm will get stretched so much that my right hand will drag on the ground like an orangutan. Or is it a gorilla? Or some kind of monkey? I'm supposed to be a genius, you'd think I'd at least know what kind of animal I'll look like when I turn into a complete freak.

And just like that, the good feelings that I had after talking to Becca and making two baskets in a row are gone.

Eight

I'm hiding out in the Saint Jude nook trying not to think about my arms. But it's impossible. If you try not to think about something, just telling yourself not to means that's all you'll be able to think about. Yep, I'm a freak. A genius with uneven arms. I can't believe it finally happened. Linc says ⅛ of an inch is nothing and to stop obsessing. Easy for him to say when his arms are the same length like a normal person.

Since I can't solve the arm problem, I figure it can't hurt to ask Saint Jude for his help with something else—even though I hope it's not a lost cause yet. And here she comes. Maya. I give Saint Jude one last tap for luck and pop out from my hiding spot, right into her path.

"Hey, Maya."

She looks at me, says nothing, and tries to walk around me. But I step right in front of her again so she can't.

"Maya, will you just listen for a minute?" She still doesn't say anything. But she doesn't try to get away, either. She stands there with her arms folded in front of her and her eyes pointing at the ceiling. "Please," I say. "Just listen."

"Fine, I'm listening." But she won't look at me. Now she's looking over my shoulder at something. Or nothing.

"Okay, well I just wanted to say I'm sorry. I don't know what for exactly, but you're really mad at me so I guess I need to be sorry for something."

Finally Maya looks at me. It's not a friendly look. "Is that supposed to be an apology?" I shrug and smile a little. "Because if it was, it was pathetic."

"Okay, how about this? I'm sorry that I scored too high on a test, and it made you mad. And that you don't want to be friends anymore." I look down at my shoes and then back up at Maya. "Because I still do." I pull at my right sleeve, making sure it covers up my 1/8 of an inch longer arm.

"You don't get it, do you?" But she looks a little less mad. She uncrosses her arms and blows her bangs out of her eyes.

"I get that you're mad. What else is there?"

Even though she was my second-best friend until six days ago, Maya is still a girl. And that means I don't know what she's talking about a lot of the time.

"You stole my thing," she says.

I raise my eyebrows in a question since I'm afraid to tell her I still don't know what she's talking about.

"I've always been the smartest one in our class," she says. "It's my thing. It's why people know who I am. I'm not good at sports, I'm not good at being friends with most of the other girls, and I'm not one of the pretty ones. But I was the smartest. And everyone knew I was the smartest. But then you stole it." Her voice doesn't sound mad anymore. It sounds sad. Which is even worse.

"Wow, maybe you're right. Maybe you're not the smartest."

Maya's head snaps up, and her mouth is in the shape of an O. I try not to laugh.

"If you're wrong about that many things, maybe you're not the smartest," I say.

"Come on, Maya, you know being smart isn't the only thing that makes you who you are. There are lots of things. It doesn't matter that you're not good at sports, most of those girls don't deserve you for a friend and, that other stuff, well that's just not true." My ears get hot when I say the last part. But it's true. Maya is pretty. Really pretty. I just try not to notice because if I do, I'm afraid I won't be able to talk to her anymore.

"So maybe I shouldn't be mad at you?" says Maya. She's almost smiling.

"Maybe not." And I do smile. "See you in G.A.S. class later?" No one else came up with a name for our class, so Cameron's horrible suggestion stuck.

"Yep, see you then."

The bell rings, telling us we're going to be late for class. We jump apart and start off in different directions. After a few steps, I turn around and see Maya looking back at me. I wave, and she sticks her tongue out, crosses her eyes, and waves back. I grin. Maybe this will be okay.

Thanks, Saint Jude.

Sister Stevie closes the door and spins around. "I've been so excited to talk to all of you. You've had a whole weekend to think about ideas for the Academic Olympics. Let's hear what you've got."

Nobody says anything at first. Then Rachel raises her hand. "Does it have to be about science?"

"Technically, yes," says Sister Stevie. "It's a science competition, but a big part of the total score is creativity. So, we should try to come up with an idea that's unusual or unexpected."

"But no poetry?" asks Rachel with a smile.

"Find a way to fit it in. That would be creative." Sister Stevie rolls the bouncy ball over and sits down. "Let's brainstorm. Nothing is off limits, and no one makes fun of anyone's suggestions. But remember we need one overall theme and then everybody will do an individual project that goes with that theme."

"How about types of extreme weather?" I say. Linc groans, but I ignore him. "We could do tornadoes, hurricanes, tsunamis, blizzards, someone could talk about climate change."

Maya looks over at me and laughs. But for the first time since last Wednesday, it's not a mean laugh. "How surprising—Gabe wants to do weather." She rolls her eyes at me. "He wants to be a meteorologist," she tells everyone. It's true. Meteorologist is on my list of possible careers. But so is a civil engineer who builds bridges and a research scientist.

"You want to be a weatherman?" says Cameron. "That's funny. I don't think you have the hair for it, though. You do *not* have TV hair."

Linc bursts out laughing. I aim my best death stare in his direction. He's supposed to be on my side. He shrugs and whispers, "Sorry, but it was funny."

"Cameron, remember the rules of brainstorming," says Sister Stevie.

"But I wasn't making fun of his idea, just his hair." Everybody laughs. Everybody except me.

"Not all meteorologists are TV weathermen," I say. "What's your brilliant idea, Cameron?"

"Well, Sister said something about systems of the body. We could do that," says Cameron.

"Yeah, but that's ordinary," says Maya. Before Sister Stevie can say anything, Maya says, "It's not a bad idea. That's not what I meant. But it's still not creative."

"Okay then, *Captain*, what do you have?" asks Cameron.

Maya has a look on her face that I've seen hundreds of times. Usually right before she scores a huge number with a word using a Q or a Z, or sometimes both, when we play Scrabble.

"Science in unexpected places," she says.

"Sounds interesting," I say. "What exactly does it mean?"

Maya looks right at me. And she talks right to me. "Well, I thought we could each come up with a place where people wouldn't expect to find science, but it's absolutely there. Like me, I could do music. Mathematics is a science, and there is a lot of math in music. And there's physics, too." Maya plays the cello so this makes sense.

"And poetry," says Rachel. "There's math in poetry." She talks louder and faster than usual. "I like your idea, Maya. A lot."

"Racing," says Ty. "I want to do racing. There's all kinds of science behind stock car racing in NASCAR." He forgets to act bored and cool for a minute.

This is actually fun. I'm not sure what I want to do, but this is fun. We're all talking and laughing and getting excited about the competition.

There's a knock at the door. Before Sister Stevie can answer it, the door opens and Mr. Dooley walks in.

"Good morning, Sister, everyone," says Mr. Dooley. "I wanted to come here to talk to my MVPs this morning."

Does Mr. Dooley think this class is some kind of sports team?

"I know Sister Stevie told you that you are going to be competing in the Academic Olympics." Mr. Dooley unbuttons the cuffs of his blue dress shirt and rolls up the sleeves, pacing back and forth in front of us. He lifts his arm to scratch his head, displaying a sweat stain in the shape of a half-moon.

"This is an outstanding opportunity for our school to make a name for myself—er—itself," Mr. Dooley says.

"We're going to be competing against a lot of schools—including Overton Prep. So I'm counting on all of you to put forth your best effort."

Overton Prep wins everything. They beat us in every sport. Even basketball. The word is that Mr. Dooley and Overton's principal, Mr. Bitterman, played tennis against each other in college. Mr. Dooley never won. Not one match. When Overton is involved, Mr. Dooley gets crazed.

"We've talked about how exciting this is, and the class has been thinking about ideas for our team's theme," says Sister Stevie. "This is a creative group so I'm sure they'll come up with something great. And Maya is our team captain."

Maya smiles at Sister Stevie and then turns her head and smiles at me. Maya's back. Maybe this genius thing doesn't have to turn everything upside down. And actually some of it's kind of cool, like being in this class and even this competition. If things with Maya are okay, and the other kids get bored with staring at me, I might even start to like being a genius.

"*Maya's* the team captain?" asks Mr. Dooley.

He says it like a question. It's not supposed to be a question. I shift in my seat and hold my breath waiting for what comes next.

"Well, I just wanted to tell all of you that I'll—er—we'll be counting on you to make us proud. And Ty, I'll be counting on you and your other team to beat Overton Prep, too."

"Okay then, thank you for coming, Mr. Dooley. We appreciate you taking the time out of your busy day, don't we?" Sister Stevie stares at the door, waiting for Mr. Dooley to leave. But he doesn't.

"Sister Stephanie, may I speak with you for a moment?"

They go out into the hallway. Oh, no. I exhale and sneak a look at Maya without actually turning my head in her direction. She's stone still, and her eyes are shiny in the way they get right before she cries. Outside the room, Mr. Dooley is doing most of the talking. I can't understand most of what he's saying, but I hear my name —a lot. Maya still doesn't move. Not a muscle. She hasn't even blinked.

"Does it even matter who the captain is?" asks Ty. "It's not like this is a real team." He mimics dribbling a basketball and taking a shot. The door opens. Mr. Dooley walks in ahead of Sister Stevie.

"So we're in agreement, Sister?" Mr. Dooley turns and looks at her. It's the first time I've seen Sister Stevie without a smile. Her jaw twitches, and she takes a breath deep enough to see.

"Yes and no, Mr. Dooley." Mr. Dooley looks surprised, like my mom does when someone doesn't agree with her about what we should have for supper. She thinks supper is her decision, and I think Mr. Dooley thinks this is his. "Maya is an excellent choice for team captain. She's organized, creative and, like *everyone* in this class, extremely bright." I keep trying to catch Maya's eye, but she won't look at me "Of course, Gabe would be a great choice as well. Science is one of his strongest subjects."

"So Gabe is going to be the team captain instead of Maya?" Ty asks.

"No, that's not what I said," says Sister Stevie. "Maya and Gabe will be co-captains."

"Co-captains. All right then," says Mr. Dooley. This time Sister Stevie takes his arm and walks him to the door, closing it close behind him.

Co-captains. Maybe this won't be so bad. I didn't want to be the captain but working with Maya will be fun. Then she turns and looks at me. And it's like our talk in the hallway never happened. We're not back to being friends. The way she looks at me makes me think we probably never will be.

Nine

"They're here," I tell Celsius and Fahrenheit. A faint glug says they're not as excited as I am. But I just heard the sound I've been waiting for—the revving of an engine.

I race Sabrina through the house and the garage, spilling out onto the driveway laughing. And there they are. My grandparents.

"Happy Thanksgiving, sweethearts." My grandma unfolds herself from her seat, pats her hair back into place, and stretches down to touch her toes. When she stands back up, she gives me a smacking kiss on my cheek and hugs me so hard I can feel my bones rub together. My grandma was a track star in college, and she still runs marathons. She hugs like she means it.

"Hi, Grandma. How was the ride?" I ask as she hands me her helmet.

"It was fine. It's a beautiful day, and Grandpa kept the ride pretty smooth," she says. My grandparents have a car. But they only drive it when it's raining or snowing. So today they came on their motorcycle. Well, motorcycle with a sidecar. My grandpa rides the motorcycle, and my grandma rides in the sidecar.

"Sabrina, look how pretty you are." Sabrina beams and twirls. She hugs my grandma and they go inside.

My grandpa turns off the motorcycle, stows his helmet, and turns to me. "My Gabe," he says and hugs me. Even if I thought I was getting too old for hugging my grandpa, it wouldn't matter. He's a hugger.

"Happy Thanksgiving, Grandpa," I say. "What's new?"

"Well, I've been working on something that's turned out to be pretty interesting. I brought some of the data to show you after supper," he says. Grandpa opens the trunk area of his motorcycle and gets out his briefcase. He never goes anywhere without it.

"I can't wait."

My grandpa is a seismologist, a scientist who studies earthquakes and movement in the earth. He specializes in glaciers, which is unbelievably cool. When he was younger, he used to travel a lot to Alaska and even once to

Antarctica to study glaciers and record changes in them. Now he's a college professor of geophysics and seismology. Regular people wouldn't think he's famous, but to people who know seismology, he's like a rock star.

He's also my hero.

My grandpa looks up at the sky, squints, and says, "Cirrus?"

"Yep," I say. "You can tell they're cirrus because they look like strands of hair."

"Strands of hair, huh? I was thinking they look like angel wings. Gabriel's wings." I roll my eyes, and my grandpa laughs. Then he puts his arm around me, and we walk in the house together.

I stop and inhale. Our house always smells good. I mean, my mom's job is baking cookies so it always smells really good. But on Thanksgiving it's like I need an extra nose to smell all the smells coming from the kitchen. Turkey, pumpkin pie, and cornbread. My stomach rumbles even though it's a while until dinner.

"Let's go see what smells so good," says my grandpa. "Has my daughter-in-law outdone herself this year?" My grandpa says this last part loud enough for my mom to hear.

We walk into the kitchen where my mom stands, apron in place, two enormous handfuls of collard greens in her hands. She gives my grandpa a cheek to kiss and then shoos us out.

"There are munchies in the family room. And Joe's in charge of drinks. So go, sit, watch football. But stay out of my kitchen."

"We're going," I say and scoot out after my grandpa.

Thanksgiving is my favorite holiday. Sabrina thinks that's weird because it's a no-present holiday, but it's my favorite. It's a whole day of eating and watching football on TV and hanging out with my grandpa. It would be perfect except for one thing. Well, three things. My cousins. They'll be here soon.

My grandpa sits in the chair with the best view of the TV, and I flop onto the floor in front of him. My dad went to get orange sodas for my grandpa and me, and Sabrina and my grandma are whispering on the other side of the room.

My grandpa clears his throat. Twice. When my grandpa clears his throat twice, it means he wants to talk to me about something. It doesn't take a genius, which I guess I am, to know what's coming.

"So Gabe, your dad told me something interesting happened last week," says my grandpa.

"Not really." I shrug. My grandpa is the person I can talk to about stuff. But I don't want to talk about finding out I'm a genius. Not even with him.

"Gabe?"

Before I can answer, the doorbell rings. My shoulders tense up at the sound. They're here. I stand up but otherwise don't move from my spot.

"Hey, Dad, hey, Gabe," says my Uncle Skip as he walks in the room, my Aunt Jennifer a few steps behind him. Uncle Skip's voice is loud, and he sounds happier to see us than he could possibly be. Instead of a hug, he shakes my grandpa's hand, and then claps me on the back so hard I almost fall over.

"Hey, Uncle Skip," I say. "Happy Thanksgiving."

"Come on in here, guys. The game's about to start," Uncle Skip yells in the direction of the hall.

And here they come. My cousins. Kyle, Kevin, and Will. Kyle's 14, Kevin's 12 like me, and Will is 10. We're not close. It's not that they're bad guys—they're fine mostly. It's just if we went to the same school, we wouldn't sit together in the cafeteria. They'd be sitting with the basketball team. Or the football team. Or the baseball team. It depends on what season it was. But the team they wouldn't be sitting with is the Academic Olympics team, that's for sure.

They come in, and the room seems too small to hold all of us. Everyone's talking and yelling over the top of each other, and my cousins drape themselves across every couch and chair.

I escape to the kitchen to beg my mom for something to do. She puts me in charge of napkins. I'm supposed to be a genius, and that's what she thinks I can do. Napkins.

"Gabe, honey, call everyone to the table." So, a promotion from napkins to messenger. I shrug and bellow, "Supper's ready," then flatten myself against the wall.

My cousins thunder in like starving buffalo, with everyone else trailing behind. There's a lot of shuffling and jostling before all the seats are filled. I close my eyes and take a giant sniff in. The perfectly Thanksgiving smells trigger my salivary glands to work overtime until I have to wipe my mouth to keep from drooling. But there's no eating. Not yet, anyway. Thanksgiving supper—or any meal—doesn't start until grace has been said. After the final "Amen," platters and bowls are passed around and around until each plate is full.

Like it is every year, my mom's Thanksgiving dinner is delicious. The cornbread melts in my mouth, the mac-'n-cheese is extra creamy and the sweet potato casserole has the perfect amount of marshmallows on top—golden brown and a tiny bit crusty. A crunch and then tangy and sweet at the same time. Yum.

For the first few minutes, the only sounds are forks on plates and murmurs of "please" and "thank you" as everyone passes platters around. Then a lot of yumming.

"So Gabe's supposed to be a genius, huh? Says who?" asks Kevin around a mouthful of turkey and gravy.

There it is. The thing I don't want to talk about with my family. But if I don't say something, my dad will.

"It was just some stupid test. It doesn't mean anything. But hey, how's basketball season going?" I ask.

"Great! We're in first place, and I'm the top scorer on the team," says Kevin. He reaches across the table and high-fives my uncle. My mom cringes as Kevin's elbow bumps into his water glass, and it tips from side to side before deciding not to topple over.

"But he's no genius, that's for sure," Kyle says. He and Will crack up.

"Ty Easterbrook, the top scorer on St. Jude's team, is in Gabe's new class. What's it called again?" says my dad.

"Greater Achieving Students," I mumble. Kyle snickers and elbows Will, who's sitting next to him.

"They call it G.A.S. class," says my sister the traitor.

I sit and wait for it. I don't have to wait long. Kevin, Kyle, and Will all make loud farting noises—Kyle and Will with their mouths, but Kevin makes his with his hands. I guess he's going for extra points for creativity. Then they all, including Sabrina, crack up. I sneak a peek at my watch to calculate just how many more minutes are left until my cousins go home. My best estimate is somewhere between 235 and 300 minutes.

"Maybe this Ty kid can give you some pointers, Gabe," says Uncle Skip.

My dad looks at me all hopeful. Does he think Ty's basketball skills are going to rub off on me if I sit next to him in class? Now's probably not a good time to tell my dad that Ty thinks he's too cool to even say "hi" to me outside of class. I stab a bite of turkey harder than I need to.

We eat until no one can manage another bite. It's back to sitting in front of the TV and waiting for the uncomfortable feeling that you get when you eat too much to go away. It takes a while.

Then, like every year, my dad stands up, adjusts the waist of his brown corduroy pants and groans. "Okay, who's up for some basketball?"

Uncle Skip, in an almost perfect imitation of my dad, stands up, adjusts the waist of his own pants, and groans. "We're in. Let's go, boys." In one movement, his three sons hop up and head outside.

"Gabe, you coming?" asks my dad.

"Sure. I'm in. And Grandpa's in too, right, Grandpa?"

"I think I'll just watch," Grandpa says with a little laugh. "I can't keep up with you boys anymore."

By the time I lace up my basketball shoes and get outside, my cousins are warming up, and the dads are making bets about who's going to beat whom. Every year the dads are the captains of the teams, and every year they make a bet. Uncle Skip is my dad's brother, and Grandma says they've been this way since they were kids. They were never on the same team. Even today, as soon as my dad sees that Uncle Skip has his Carolina State jacket on, he heads back in for his University of Carolina sweatshirt—and hat. Finally, we're ready to start.

"Rock, paper, scissors for who picks first," says Uncle Skip.

"Fine," says my dad. "One, two, three, shoot."

My dad throws "rock," and Uncle Skip throws "scissors."

"My pick," says my dad. "I pick Kyle."

Kyle is always the first pick. He's the oldest and the tallest and the best basketball player. I tell myself I don't care that my dad didn't pick me first, and I mostly don't. Mostly. He'll pick me on his next turn.

"I'll take Kevin," says Uncle Skip. He and Kevin high-five and whoop. Loudly.

It's my dad's turn again. He looks at me and then at Will. Then he looks down at the ground. "I'll take Will."

"Huh?" says Will. His eyes dart back and forth between

my dad and me. "Uh, okay." And he walks over to stand with Kyle and my dad. My dad.

What just happened? Did my dad actually not pick me for his team? Seriously? I'm standing here alone, the last guy to get picked. And my own dad did it to me.

I feel a tickle behind my eyes that means I might start to cry. I bite my lip—hard—until the feeling goes away. In its place is something else. Something worse.

Uncle Skip, Aunt Jennifer and the boys are gone, and my grandpa and I are in my room working on my suspension bridge. Something's not quite right; it's kind of sagging in the middle. After we take a few measurements, I get out my box of spare LEGO pieces, and we start building another support.

When the knock on my door comes, I'm half expecting it.

"Come in." I don't bother to turn around.

"Hey, Champ," says my dad.

"Don't call me that," I say under my breath. I still don't turn around. Instead, I add three LEGO pieces to the left side of the bridge, cock my head to the right, and take them off again.

"You're not upset about the game, are you? Mom

thinks you're upset that I didn't pick you for my team."

Mom thinks? I don't say anything. I just shrug and grunt.

"I told her you understand how it is with me and Uncle Skip. I couldn't let him win again this year."

"Okay," I say. Even though it's not.

"See, I told Mom you were okay," says my dad. "Have fun playing with Grandpa."

He didn't seem to notice that I never looked at him. That I never even turned around.

My grandpa sighs and squeezes my hand. "He didn't mean to hurt your feelings. He really doesn't know." Another squeeze, tighter this time.

I look up at my grandpa and see his usually smiling mouth is turned down at the edges, and his shoulders are slumped. Telling him how I feel about what happened with my dad will only make my grandpa sad. And I don't want to make him sad.

"Hey, Grandpa, can you show me what you've been working on? You know, the stuff that you said is getting interesting." I force my mouth into a smile.

My grandpa reaches over and pats my cheek.

"You got it. Just wait until you see this." He grabs a file with a bunch of graphs and pictures. After a few minutes, I know a lot more about earthquakes on glaciers.

"Wow, that's incredible," I say. "How did you figure all that out?"

"The same way you would. I used my brain." He waits until I look up from the pictures. "Being given a brain like yours or mine is a gift. It's a talent just like being a great athlete or musician."

I look at my grandpa and raise my eyebrows. Being smart isn't a talent, is it? And if it is a gift, I wonder if I could return it for something better. Something like being tall or good at basketball or talking to girls. But since gifts from God aren't exactly the same thing as getting an ugly sweater for Christmas, I'm pretty sure I can't trade mine in.

"God gave you a talent," Grandpa says again. "And just like having musical talent or athletic talent, you need to use it—not just for yourself. I'm proud of you, Gabe. You are a gift. All of you, including your brain and your less than stellar jump shot." He laughs at his own joke and then his face turns serious. "You need to be proud of you, too." Something about what my grandpa says sounds a lot like what Sister Stevie says about being a gift.

"Got it." And I do. Sort of. "Is it okay if I think about it later, though? I want to see more about the glaciers."

My grandpa smiles at me and pulls out another slide. "Okay, this was the most exciting thing we found last week." I lean over until our heads nearly touch and let my grandpa take me away to the glaciers.

But there's a corner of my brain that's still thinking about my dad. About how he didn't pick me for his team. And about what that really means.

Ten

Since it's the first day back after Thanksgiving break, maybe I'll get lucky. Here goes: 34 right, 4 left, 16 right. Listen for the click and lift. Nothing. It doesn't open. Again. Sigh. Slump. I don't think even Saint Jude can help with this lost cause. I straighten my shoulders, grab the handle of my backpack, and head off to class.

"I'm sorry. Excuse me, I'm really sorry," I say as I smack my backpack into the shin of a girl going in the other direction. She rolls her eyes, does that thing girls do where they flip their hair over their shoulders, and then giggles with her friend.

Ever since I discovered my right arm is $\frac{1}{8}$ inch longer than my left, I've been trying to pull my backpack with my left arm. So far, it's not working.

When I walk into G.A.S. class, Maya is already there.

"Hey, Maya," I say.

She looks straight ahead and acts like she can't hear me.

"How was your Thanksgiving?"

Still nothing.

"Did your mom make *plátanos machos*?"

Plátanos machos are Mexican fried bananas, and they're the best things I've ever eaten—not that I'd tell my mom that. They're crunchy and sweet and taste a little bit like orange. Mrs. Ling makes them for every holiday and always makes sure there are enough for me when I sneak over after my family leaves. I knew Maya wouldn't have been happy to see me this year, so I didn't go. If things weren't weird and I had gone, I would've told her about my dad not picking me for his team. But things are weird so I didn't.

"I'm ignoring you," says Maya through clenched teeth. Nothing but her mouth moves.

"Yeah, I noticed. But you shouldn't be. I'm sorry Mr. Dooley wanted me to be a captain. I didn't want to be captain—you should be."

"I know." She finally looks at me. "And it's another thing you ruined. I'm not speaking to you. So please stop talking to me." At least she's being polite about it.

I put my hands up in front of me. "Okay. You win."

I sit down next to Linc.

"She's still mad, huh?"

Linc's rooting around in his backpack. Something tells me he's looking for his homework. The rooting speeds up, which makes me think the homework might not be in there.

"Yep. And I think it's the long-lasting kind of mad this time." Maya gets mad easily, but it usually goes away just as fast. Not this time.

"Aha!" Linc pulls out a wrinkled piece of paper with a smear of something that looks like ketchup or grape jelly on it. It's his homework assignment. He puts it on his desk and tries to iron it with his hand. I get my assignment out of my G.A.S. class green folder and place it on my desk. Linc looks over at my unwrinkled paper, looks back at his, laughs, and shrugs.

"Everybody stand up," says Sister Stevie.

Chairs screech as everyone pushes back and stands up.

"Okay, now hands up over your heads."

"Why?" asks Ty. "What are we doing?"

"Hands over your heads," Sister Stevie says again.

I put mine up over my head, so do Linc, Cameron, Maya, and Rachel. Sister Stevie waits. Ty grumbles and then finally puts his up as well.

"Now stretch to the right. Go ahead, go to the right as far as you can."

This is weird. I like Sister Stevie, but this is weird even for her. Linc looks at me, grins, and stretches. I cross my eyes and stretch, too. Then somebody lets out a fart that sounds like it comes from a rhinoceros. And it's not me.

"Cameron, that's disgusting," says Maya. She stops stretching to turn away from him and hold her nose. Cameron cracks up.

"Okay, everybody sit down," says Sister Stevie.

More chair scraping and we're all back in our seats. Sister Stevie sits and then bounces on the blue ball a few times.

"Why did I have you do that?" she asks.

"So Cameron could work out his gas bubble?" says Linc. Maya's still holding her nose. Whatever vapor trail there was didn't make it all the way over here.

"Are you going to tell us or make us guess?" asks Ty.

"I'll tell you, Ty. I had you stretch to the right because we're going to work on stretching the right side of your brains."

Clever, but I don't know what it means.

"How are we going to do that?" asks Linc.

"Poetry," says Sister Stevie. "We're going to do that through reading, discussing, and writing poetry."

Did she say *writing* poetry?

"In fact, entire books of the Bible are poetry. Does anyone know which ones?"

"Psalms?" says Rachel.

Sister nods.

"And the book of Job in the original language." Maya answers without looking up from picking away at her thumbnail.

"You're both right. As a matter of fact, the Book of Psalms consists of 150 poems. Reading through some of them or other books of poetry is a great way to find inspiration for this assignment."

"I don't write poetry. I play basketball." I wonder again why Ty is in this class. He acts like he doesn't to want to be here.

"But you will write poetry, Ty," says Sister Stevie. "You all will. I think you'll surprise yourselves." She smiles at Ty and then looks at each of us. "Rachel reads poetry. Can you tell us about why you enjoy it?"

Rachel looks up and then back down. She fiddles with the pages of the book of poetry that's always on her desk.

"Poetry is magic," she says. "It's painting with words. Each poem is like art." Her words trail off at the end.

Sister Stevie nods. "Exactly. That's why I love it, too."

Rachel's cheeks turn pink, and the corners of her mouth turn up in a private smile. That's more than she usually says in class. She tucks her curly brown hair behind her ears and looks down at her desk.

"If poetry's magic, then I want to be a magician," says Linc. He acts like he's waving a wand around. Everyone laughs.

"Well, Linc, I'll do my best to teach you some magic tricks. To teach all of you how to create your own magic," says Sister Stevie. "Because you're each going to write an original poem and recite it to the class next week. We're going to have our very own poetry jam." She puts her arms out to the sides and smiles wide.

"What's a poetry jam?" My voice cracks on the last word.

"It's a performance, people reciting their work. A poetry *slam* is a competition, but you're not competing with each other so ours will be a *jam*." Sister Stevie looks at me, and she must be able to see the panic on my face because she says, "It'll be fun, Gabe. Really."

Fun? No way is this going to be fun. My ears burn, and I have a tingling feeling in my fingers and toes. I clutch my Superman pen in my hand and send out an S.O.S. to Saint Jude. It doesn't help. If I feel this anxious just thinking about reading a poem to the class, what's it going to be like when I actually do it? My stomach twists and clenches in answer. This time it's me who sends out a gas cloud. A silent gas cloud.

I count to ten and wait to see if anyone notices.

"Cameron!" says Maya. "Stop it." She plugs her nose again.

"I didn't do anything," says Cameron.

Maya rolls her eyes and huffs. I feel bad about letting Cameron take the blame, but only for a minute.

"What's the poem supposed to be about?" asks Linc.

"Anything you want." Sister Stevie fiddles with her veil and smiles one of those no-teeth smiles. "Maybe one of you will write your own psalm. You see, poetry is best when you write about something that you feel strongly about, something that's important or beautiful to you."

Linc turns and looks at Rachel, then he looks at me. I can almost hear his brain working and see the light bulb over his head. He has an idea. A plan.

When I get to our table in the cafeteria, Linc's already there plowing through his lunch. As soon as I sit down, he starts talking.

"This is it. This is my in. Poetry. Why didn't I think of that before? She has that poetry book with her every day. I'll woo her with poetry. It's genius. Well, not like your kind of genius, but still, genius." Linc is talking so fast I can hardly keep up.

"Rachel?" I ask.

"Of course, Rachel. I told you I'd figure out how to make her fall for me. I'm going to write her a love poem." His chin in his hand, Linc stares across the cafeteria to where Rachel sits with her friends. "Look at her. She's so beautiful."

"Do you think that's a good idea?"

Linc's my friend, my best friend, so I should support him. But being a good friend also means trying to save your friend, your best friend, from making a total fool of himself. And I have a feeling that's where this is going to end.

"What do you mean? Of course, it's a good idea. She's beautiful, she loves poetry, and I want to woo her."

"Woo her?" I ask. "Who says 'woo'? Where did you hear that anyway? Have you been reading your mom's romance novels again?" Linc gets bored sometimes when he's home alone.

"You were supposed to forget I told you about that," says Linc. "But since we're talking about wooing, you need to figure out how to woo Becca."

"I'm not wooing Becca." It comes out louder than I

meant it to. I look around to make sure no one heard. I can't believe I just said that.

"But you should be. Seriously, you need to think about how you can woo her. Maybe you should write a love poem, too."

"Shut up. Shut up. Shut up about wooing, and shut up about poetry."

Linc opens his mouth to say something else, and I throw a french fry at him. And he does shut up. For now.

Eleven

Bike helmet strapped on, I get on my bike and start pedaling down the street, in the opposite direction from school. Each block I pass, the houses and the yards get bigger, and everything gets quieter. The last block is where Linc's house is. But I don't turn into his driveway. I keep going. At the end of the street is a sort of path that is really just beaten down grass. The path leads down to a creek. I stop at the bank of the creek and flop onto the damp ground.

I was right. We've had enough rain lately for the creek to be perfect for skipping stones. I look around and find a handful of good ones. Using the motion that my grandpa first taught me when I was six, I skip the first stone—

four bounces. Not bad, but not good either. I try again. Sidearm toss with a sharp flick of my wrist—six bounces. Better.

Speed, spin, and angle. I try to remember everything my grandpa taught me about skipping. It's science. Physics mostly. You get more skips if you get the speed and spin just right. That's the toss and the flick. And some scientist actually figured out that to get the most skips possible—the world record is fifty-one—the stone should hit the water at a twenty-degree angle. Good to know, but I have no idea how to make that happen.

Here goes—this time nine skips. Personal best.

Last summer I brought Maya and Linc here and taught them how to skip stones. I tried to tell them all about the science behind it, but Linc thought learning the science somehow took the fun out of it. Maya got it—and got the most bounces—ten!

The science in skipping stones. Could that be my project for the Academic Olympics? It would be unexpected. But would it be good enough?

After Mr. Dooley came in and ruined everything by making me Maya's co-captain, everyone just agreed with her idea of "Science in Unexpected Places." I hoped that would make her happy. It didn't. She's still not talking to me.

So Maya's mad at me. And that's probably not going to change. I've tried to talk to her. I've tried to make her see that it's no big deal. But now I'm starting to get mad back. She's blaming me and being mean to me about something that's not my fault. I didn't do anything. I didn't do anything wrong, and I lost a friend anyway. My second-best friend.

I stare at the trees on the other side of the creek. There are only a couple brown leaves hanging onto the end of the branches.

Maya and I used to come here and climb those trees. The big one on the left was the easiest, but the one next to it was more fun. Of course, she always climbed higher than me.

I know my parents are excited about me being a genius and getting all this attention. I guess it makes them proud. And I know my grandpa said it's a gift from God and that I need to be proud of myself. But to me, it doesn't seem that great. The stuff that was hard for me before is still hard for me. Like girls. And being shortish. And my dad.

Ever since he didn't pick me for his team on Thanksgiving, my dad has been acting weird. Too happy and way too much like he's my buddy. It's driving me crazy. I know he's sorry or something, but every time he acts weird, it makes me think about it all over again. And every time I do, I feel crummy about it all over again.

Why can't he understand that I like sports? I like watching sports and even playing basketball for fun. But I'm not good at sports. And that's okay with me. But it doesn't seem like it's okay with him. I wish I could make him see that there's more to sports than just being tall or strong or super-coordinated.

Like in basketball, you have to really think about distance and angles. And in baseball, you need to think about speed and force. There's all kinds of physics just in throwing a pitch. And golf, which my dad loves but isn't very good at, there's science in every part of golf. But my dad only thinks about the body.

Maybe it's because that's what he does in his job. That's what a physical therapist does—he works with the body. I wish I could make him see that there's more to sports than just the body.

Wait. I slap my hand on the ground and scare a tiny frog that was hanging out on a leaf next to me. He jumps high in the air once and then hops away. Sorry, little guy, but I just had an idea. Maybe even a genius idea.

Can I do my project on sports? Can I show my dad— and Ty Easterbrook and everyone else who thinks being good at sports is the most important thing—that sports are really about science? That understanding the science of a sport could actually make you better at that sport?

I lie back on the cool, damp ground and look up at the sky. If I ignore the wet spot growing on the butt of my jeans, it's a perfect spot for cloud watching. Altostratus clouds block most of the sun, but a few rays shine through some thin spots and seem to reach for the ground. They're the kind of rays that make you think about heaven—like it's right there. Like maybe God hears you and, if you listen with more than just your ears, even answers back once in a while.

"Tomorrow's the deadline for sending in our entry," says Maya. "So I need to know right now what each of you decided on for your project. I'm doing mine on the math and science of music." The way she says it lets us know that it's decided and that she wouldn't welcome any questions.

Maya stands at the front of the classroom, notebook open and pen ready to write. It's the pen I gave her for her twelfth birthday—the blue one with the musical note charm that dangles from the top. I wonder if she remembers it was from me. I wonder if she remembers I'm supposed to be the co-captain.

"Cameron, you're first," she says. "What's your project?"

"I'm going to do the science of humor," says Cameron. Maya raises an eyebrow and motions with her hand to tell him to keep talking. "Well, there's a lot of science behind why people think things are funny and what makes people laugh. It's mostly brain stuff. So that's what I'm doing."

That's interesting. And creative. And it's Cameron's idea. Hmmm.

Maya's face changes. She smiles. "That's actually a really good idea. I like it." She writes it down in her notebook.

Rachel's getting her wish. She's going to do her project on the mathematics of poetry. And Ty is sticking with his idea about the science behind NASCAR.

That leaves Linc and me. And Linc wouldn't tell me what he decided. But he was giggling like a girl when he wouldn't tell me. That worries me.

Maya slowly turns her head and looks at Linc. Her eyes are like lasers.

"Linc, I can hardly wait to hear your idea," she says.

Sister Stevie clears her throat.

Maya pastes a fake smile on her face. "Really, can't wait. So, what is it?"

Linc sits up straight and grins. "The science of love." He says it in some cheesy late-night radio DJ voice and then looks around to make sure everyone heard him.

"What?" says Maya. I know what she's thinking.

She thinks Linc is messing around. That he's not taking this seriously on purpose. See, Maya and Linc are—or were—my two best friends. But they aren't each other's best friends. If it wasn't for me, they would never have been friends at all. Because they are—I mean were—my two best friends, they tolerate each other. Kind of how positive charges and negative charges in clouds tolerate each other. But just like the negative charge in a cloud can interact with the positive charge and cause lightning, I always know that with Linc and Maya we're always one spark away from a thunderstorm.

"Linc, I'm not sure that's an appropriate choice," says Sister Stevie.

"Oh, don't worry. It'll be PG—I promise, strictly PG and middle-school appropriate," says Linc. "I'm talking about the chemistry of love—you know chemicals in the brain and stuff like that. Maybe a few hormones." He's talking fast and smiling big and his cheeks are pink. Then he glances over at Rachel and that's when I know. It's part of the plan. Part of the woo.

"We'll talk more about this Linc. That leaves Gabe," says Sister Stevie. "I'm sure you and Maya have already discussed your idea, since you're leading the team together." The way she says it tells me she doesn't think this at all. "But why don't you tell the rest of us what you decided."

"Sports," I say.

Ty looks at me and snorts under his breath. "You're doing your project on sports?"

I look right at him. "Yes, I am. The science of sports. My project will be about how there are no sports without science. And how people like you could get better at your chosen sport if you took the time to understand the science behind it."

Ty doesn't say anything. But Maya does. "Sounds fine," she says and writes it down in her notebook. Maya's eyes are big in her face, and she's biting her lip to keep from smiling.

The Maya who was my second-best friend until last month would have been happy that I stood up for myself like that. She would have cheered me on. This new Maya can't do that—won't do that. But she wants to smile. I know she does.

Sister Stevie rubs her hands together like she's trying to get them warm. "This is so exciting! Everyone's ideas sound spectacular, and I can't wait to see what each of you comes up with."

"But there's something else I'm really looking forward to. Don't forget our class poetry jam is on Wednesday. Each of you will read the poem you've written aloud." Sister clasps her hands in front of her. "It's going to be so much fun!"

Fun? I don't see how. Maybe my mind does need to be stretched. But writing a poem and reading it to the class. How can that be anything but a disaster?

Twelve

I've just swallowed my last gulp of orange juice when it starts.

"Okay, who wants to go first?" my dad asks.

"Me. I'm first," says Sabrina. "The shrimp can wait."

Sabrina flounces past me and stands next to the door that leads to the backyard. That's where my dad has been marking our heights since we were old enough to stand up. And it's where I can see the date last summer when Sabrina passed me.

Right after it happened, my mom went on and on about growth spurts and puberty and how girls' growth spurts happen earlier than boys' growth spurts. The whole thing was embarrassing—I mean just hearing my mom say the word puberty was excruciating—and not at all helpful. Because the only thing that mattered was that my younger sister was taller than me. And she still is.

I can see Sabrina stretching herself as tall as possible, like there's a string pulling her head up. My dad takes his pencil and makes a mark at the top of her head. She steps aside, and he says, "Looks like it's the same as last month. Five feet one inch."

Sabrina harrumphs. "Bet you didn't grow either."

I stare out the window and pretend I don't hear her.

"Come on, Gabe, you're up," says my dad.

Okay. So Sabrina didn't grow. But did I? Well, my right arm did, but what about the rest of me?

"Make sure you flatten his hair down, Dad," says Sabrina. "It's not fair if you let his puffy hair count." My dad chuckles and flattens down my hair, which by the way is exactly like his hair. The pencil skitters across my scalp as he makes the mark.

Sabrina goes up on her toes and starts twirling or something around the kitchen.

"Hey, Champ. You grew."

Sabrina stops twirling so abruptly that she has to grab onto the counter to keep from falling over. "What? He did not. No way."

I step away from the door and look. Sure enough, the fresh mark is higher than the one from last month.

"Yep, a whole inch. Gabe's up to five feet," says my dad. "You did it. You're finally five feet tall." He puts his hand up for a high five. I smile and give him one.

I grew an entire inch. And Sabrina didn't. Now she's only one inch taller than me. My right arm may be longer than my left but still, I'm five feet tall.

"Okay guys, I can do this. I mean, I talk to her when I'm tutoring her. And sometimes it's not just about math. So, I should be able to talk to her now, right?"

Fahrenheit blows a bubble that rises to the top of the bowl, and Celsius swims to the surface to get some food. They don't seem to be agreeing with me, but they're not exactly disagreeing either.

Breathe in, breathe out, and open the door. I walk to the kitchen, following the smell of fresh cookies and the sound of giggling. Sabrina and Becca, of course. They're always giggling. Sabrina's giggle is annoying. It gets inside my head and bounces around until it actually makes my brain hurt. But Becca's giggle sounds like music—it's like wind chimes. I push the swinging door open and walk in.

"Look at this, Gabe—look!" says Becca. She comes flying across the kitchen toward me, waving a piece of paper.

My feet turn to cement, and my mind turns to mush. She's smiling, and her nose is all crinkly and . . . mush.

"I got a B+. I really did, a B+!"

She's holding the paper out, and I finally snap out of it enough to reach for it. It's a math test. And right below her name is a big red B+ with a smiley face after it.

"Wow, that's great." I make myself look right at her and smile. "That's really great."

"I know, right? I couldn't believe it, and I don't think Mr. McCoy could believe it either. But I did it. And it's all because you helped me. See, you really are a genius. Thank you, thank you, thank you!"

And before I know what's happening, she's hugging me. Becca Piccarelli is hugging me. I just stand there with my left arm hanging at my side and my right arm still stretched out holding onto her math test.

"Hey, guys, what's going on?"

Great, Linc's here. And Becca is still hugging me.

"Hey, Linc," says Becca. She squeezes one more time and takes a step back. "I was just showing Gabe I got a B+ on my math test, and it's all because of him."

"Really?" Linc looks at me and raises his eyebrows. I just shrug.

"Yep. He's been tutoring me, and it just started making sense."

Sabrina snorts under her breath.

"It's true, Sabrina. He's a really good tutor, you should have him help you."

"No way," says Sabrina.

"Not gonna happen," I say at the same time.

"Well, anyway, my mom is going to want you to tutor me forever," says Becca. "My dad, too. I hope you don't mind." And she looks right at me and smiles. And giggles. There it goes again. Mush.

"Congratulations, Becca. And I'm glad Gabe's doing a good job," says my mom. "Now who's ready to taste some cookies?"

The four of us climb onto the counter stools and get ready. Sabrina's still mad that I grew, and she didn't, and probably other stuff too, so she won't sit next to me. I end up between Becca and Linc.

My mom takes these tastings very seriously. Whenever she wants to introduce new flavors to her Heavenly Bites clients, she has us test them first. And since my mom treats it like a real job, she even pays us. I'd do it for free, but I don't tell her that.

"Today you'll be testing three new flavors." My mom is wearing a Heavenly Bites apron and passes out Heavenly Bites notepads and pens for us to use in our scoring.

"That's okay, Mom, I'll use my own pen." I take my

Superman pen out of my pocket and hold it for a minute. Maybe it'll help me get through sitting with my elbow in touching distance of Becca's elbow.

My mom passes out the first new flavor—she calls them "Happy Yule Y'all Bars." They're some kind of gingerbread with white frosting. And Mom's right—they taste like Christmas. Yum.

"Still with the lucky pen, huh?" says Linc. "I don't get it. Is it supposed to make you feel like Superman? Or does it have special powers?"

"Shut up, Linc," I say through teeth gritted into a fake smile. "You know, there's probably a reason Superman never had a sidekick."

Linc laughs and a few crumbs of cookie come flying out of his mouth.

"I think it's cute that he has a lucky pen," says Becca.

Did she say *cute*?

I start to take a sip of milk to wash down the hunk of gingerbread that's suddenly stuck in my throat. The cup is halfway to my mouth when Linc elbows me in the side so hard that I fall off my stool. As I lie on my back like a turtle with milk dripping off my face, I'm sure of it. Superman was right.

"Did you hear what she said? Did you? She said that you're cute. She actually said the word 'cute,'" says Linc. He sits on my bed, then stands up and then sits back down. "I don't believe it."

From the spot where I stand changing out of my milk-soaked shirt, I reach for a pillow from my bed and throw it at Linc. It actually hits the mark and knocks the baseball hat off his head.

"Why'd you do that?"

"To shut you up, that's why." I groan. "Those cookies were so good, I ate too many." I actually think about unbuttoning my jeans like my dad sometimes does after dinner.

"And you want to shut me up why? Becca said you were cute. Becca. The girl you have a crush on. I'm just repeating what she said. Isn't this a good thing? Don't you want her to think you're cute?"

"She said it was cute that I have a lucky pen. That's different than saying that *I'm* cute. And even if it isn't, it was more cute like a puppy is cute than cute like a guy you'd want to hang out with."

Because it was like that, wasn't it? She didn't really mean that she thinks I'm cute. She couldn't think that. Could she?

"She said 'cute,'" says Linc. "And now it's up to you to

woo. Come on, Gabe, woo already."

"I'm not going to woo. And seriously, you've got to stop reading your mom's books. It's not good."

"I'm writing a love poem for Rachel. I'm taking action. Girls like guys who take action." Linc flops backward on my bed and stares at a spot on the ceiling. "This poem I'm writing for Rachel is going to work. Trust me. I'm right about this. Action."

"Are you sure you want to do this?" I say. "I kind of have a bad feeling about it." Which isn't exactly the truth. I don't kind of have a bad feeling. I positively have a terrible feeling. But the smile on his face says Linc doesn't even hear me.

Thirteen

Why do palms sweat when you're nervous? I mean you expect your armpits might sweat. That's what armpits do. But why the palms of your hands, which never sweat any other time?

Now's not the time to solve that mystery, because now's almost the time to get up in front of the G.A.S. class and recite my poem. The poem I wrote that my hands may or may not be too sweaty and slippery to hold onto.

Sister Stevie starts to write on the board. She hasn't said anything yet. This is weird; she's always saying something. She writes:

"I praise you, for I am fearfully and wonderfully made.

Wonderful are your works; that I know very well." Psalm 139:14 Um, does that mean that I should be afraid of how God made me or that how he made me is a good thing? That last part makes it sound like I should know, but I don't. Great.

Sister Stevie isn't done yet. Under the psalm, she jots something else.

Emotion . . . thought . . . words.

"Robert Frost said that poetry is the result of feelings finding thoughts, and thoughts expressing themselves in words."

Huh? I'm sure my poem doesn't do any of that. My stomach clenches.

Sister Stevie turns around and smiles one of those smiles with no teeth. It's the kind of smile you'd have after waking up from a good dream.

"Welcome to our first poetry jam," she says. "Who wants to kick us off?"

"I'll go," says Cameron. "I wrote a limerick." He saunters to the front of the room, takes a peek at his paper, and chuckles.

"In a nook there stands a stone dude.
They say his name is Saint Jude.
I walked by and did pause.
He said, 'You're a lost cause.'
And I said, 'Hey, man, that's rude.'"

There's a small silence and then Sister Stevie looks up at the ceiling, opens her mouth wide, and guffaws. Then the rest of the class laughs, too.

"Well done, Cameron," says Sister Stevie. "What a perfect example of humor in poetry."

Cameron beams and sits down.

I was hoping that my poem would at least be better than Cameron's. I didn't think someone who cracks jokes all the time could write a poem. But he did. He just found a way to be funny and do it.

Next up is Maya. She stands straight and as tall as she can, which isn't very tall, and starts talking. It doesn't take long, and no one understands a word.

"Maya?" says Sister Stevie. There are a lot of questions in that one word.

Maya turns toward Sister Stevie and says, "It's a haiku. It's in Mandarin. Here's the translation. It's seventeen syllables in Mandarin like it's supposed to be, but not when it's translated. I choose not to translate it for the class."

She hands Sister Stevie a slip of paper and sits down.

A haiku recited in Mandarin? Really? That's over the top even for Maya. And why won't she tell us what it says? Sister Stevie reads it, and a line appears between her eyebrows. Maya sits with her arms crossed around her middle and stares straight ahead.

Next, Rachel gets up and reads something that goes on for a really long time and doesn't rhyme at all. She says it's called free verse, and it can be whatever you want it to be. I don't get how that's a poem. But Sister Stevie goes crazy over it so I guess it must be.

Ty's poem is about basketball. And he rhymes "dribble" with "quibble" and "rebound" with "astound." Seriously.

Linc told me he wants to go last, so it's my turn. Poem in hand, I walk to the front of the room. When I peek at everyone's faces, I see that Maya is staring blankly at me, Cameron is making some kind of stupid face, and Ty isn't looking at me at all. He's messing with the bottom of his shoe. Linc's still gazing at Rachel so he's no help.

I decide to pick a spot on the back wall and talk to it. My mom taught me that trick the first time I had to give a speech. It worked in fourth grade. Let's hope it works now.

"An ode is a poem written in praise or honor of something. Mine is called 'An Ode to Ology.'" I look down at my poem and start to read.

"In science there are many ologies.
The study of life is biology .
If it's the moon that you like, there's selenology.
Named for an angel? Then try angelology.
Caves are fun to explore and so is saying
speleology.

For the heat and eruption of volcanoes,
   it's volcanology.
Then cool it down through the study of water,
   hydrology.
Of all the ologies it's true,
I have favorites, but only two.
The first is studied by my grandfather—seismology.
And the second is a hobby of mine—meteorology.
So if it's science you might be interested in
Pick an ology and take it for a spin."

I did it. My ears are so hot they feel like they're on fire, and I think I forgot to breathe, but at least I got through to the end without fainting or farting.

Without looking at anyone, I turn and hand my poem to Sister Stevie. She opens her mouth to say something, when I hear Cameron's voice.

"Did you really write a poem about science?" he asks.

I turn to look at him. "Yeah."

He snickers. "Okay, just checking. Was it like a love poem or something?"

I stand there not saying anything. Cameron is such a jerk sometimes.

"Cameron, that's not how we do things in this class," says Sister Stevie. "You wrote a poem about something that you feel strongly about—humor. And it was good.

Gabe wrote about science, which is something he feels strongly about. And his poem was good, too."

Nobody else says anything. Is it because they agree with Cameron? I trudge back to my seat and stare out the window, waiting to see what Linc's going to do.

When Linc clears his throat, I turn to look at him. He's already standing in front and is ready to go. I check for signs of nervousness. Nothing. His hands holding the poem are steady. His face isn't red. He's not even fidgeting, and Linc always fidgets. He looks perfectly calm. And he's looking right at Rachel and smiling.

Linc starts to talk. "Sister Stevie talked about poetry being a way to express your feelings about something beautiful. So that's what I did. I wrote an acrostic, where the first letter of each line spells out a person's name.

"R is for your radiant smile

A is for your artistry with words

C is for your charismatic personality

H is because you're heavenly to look at

E is for your effervescence

L is because you're lovely through and through."

He said he was going to do it. He said he wanted to woo. And take action.

I could see the exact moment that Rachel figured out the poem was about her. It was when Linc said the letter

H. The redness started at the neck of her shirt and spread higher and higher up her face until it disappeared into her hair. I bet if I look closely, even her scalp is blushing. But she's smiling a little, too.

Not even Sister Stevie breaks this silence. Linc walks over and gives the poem, the neatly written poem on uncrinkled paper, to Rachel. Then he sits down.

After what seems like a long time when no one speaks or even moves, Sister Stevie stands up and says, "Linc, do you have a copy for me?"

He chuckles, digs around in his bag, and finds a crumpled paper with a bunch of words crossed out and rewritten. This is what he turns in as his assignment.

Before Sister Stevie can say anything, the door opens, and a student walks in and hands Sister Stevie a note. She reads it and then says, "Linc, Mrs. Capistrano has asked to see you. Take your things with you."

I don't think I've moved or even breathed since Linc finished. He's my best friend. So it's going to be my job to help put the pieces of him back together.

Then just before he gets to the door, Linc turns around, looks at me, and raises his hand in a kind of wave. He's smiling.

After Linc's mysterious summons to Mrs. Capistrano's office, he was gone for the rest of the day. No Linc at lunch. No Linc waiting at my locker at the end of the day. So I'm sitting on my front steps rolling a basketball out and back with my foot while I wait to see if he'll show up for our regular game of H-I-P-P-O-P-O-T-A-M-U-S.

I'm also practicing my pep talk. Because even though Linc was smiling after he read his poem to the class, he has to have figured out what a disaster it was. It was such a disaster that not even Cameron made a joke. Nobody said anything. But when the bell rang, I saw Rachel look at the poem again and then fold it in half very carefully and put it in her backpack.

I'm staring at the ground thinking about the fact that my butt is freezing and I should really stand up when I hear a whoop. I look up and see Linc flying down the street on his bike. He's standing up on the pedals, face turned to the sky. Just when I'm sure he's about to crash, he looks down, makes a sharp turn into my driveway, screeches to a stop, and almost flies off his bike. When his helmet comes off, I can see I wasted my time working on a pep talk.

Linc's smile reaches from one ear to the other and shows pretty much every tooth in his mouth.

"Hey," I say. It's more of a question than a hi. "So where'd you go today?"

"Mrs. C. wanted to talk to me about the usual—my motivation—and then I had to go to the orthodontist. Let's play," says Linc. "I feel lucky."

He kicks the ball out from under my foot, grabs it and starts dribbling toward the basket. Woomp, woomp, woomp. He stops and takes a shot from way outside, beyond where three-point range would be. And he makes it.

Linc turns to me and grins. "Told you. Today I'm lucky." Then he runs after the ball and passes it to me.

Even though I have never made a shot from this range and probably will never make a shot from this range, I go through my routine. I close my eyes and try to see myself making the shot. Woomp, woomp, woomp. Stop, aim, and shoot. Air ball.

"I guess you're not feeling lucky today, huh?" says Linc. "That's H."

He's laughing at *me*. After what happened in G.A.S. class today. Seriously?

"So, you're in a good mood. Any special reason?" I say.

"What do you mean? You were there. It was awesome." Linc plucks the ball out of my mom's flowers. He spins it on his finger, then takes it, and shoots. Another impossible shot made. "I did it, Gabe. I wooed her. I said I would, and I did."

When the ball comes to me, I grab it and hold on. "Yeah, you did it. But did you think it went well? 'Cuz I kind of didn't think so."

"What do you mean?" Linc looks at me like I'm the crazy one. "It went great."

Okay, I'll have to try another way. "Um, did you think Rachel liked it?"

"I don't know. She looked pretty embarrassed so maybe not. But that wasn't the point."

"Now I'm totally confused. Explain please. I thought the whole point was to woo Rachel and get her to fall in love with you. So if her liking it wasn't the point, what was?"

Linc looks at me, shakes his head, and pats me on the shoulder.

"I feel sorry for you," he says. "You just don't get it. And you're supposed to be the genius."

I give him a look—eyebrows up—and shake his hand off my shoulder.

"Okay, okay, don't get mad. What I mean is, Rachel Zimmerman liking me was not the point. I mean, she's Rachel Zimmerman. And I'm me."

"Then, why'd you do it? Why'd you set yourself up for that?"

"Because I had to. She's the most beautiful girl in

school. And she's right there in our class. And so I did something. I took action. And it felt incredible. Right after I read the poem, I swear I felt like I could fly."

I open my mouth to say something but, before I can, I hear giggling. Two giggles. One grating, the other musical. Sabrina and Becca. I turn around, and there they are, walking up the sidewalk.

"Oh my gosh, Linc, we heard about what you did today," says Sabrina. "The poem you wrote for Rachel. I can't believe you did that. It's so romantic."

"Romantic," says Becca, like an echo. She's clutching her hands in front of her and looking at Linc with her eyes all big. "I hope somebody writes a poem like that for me one day."

"Everyone was talking about it at lunch," says Sabrina. "All the girls think it's so sweet."

Still giggling, they go inside.

Linc looks at me and smirks. "You heard what she said. It's romantic. Action, Gabe, you've got to take action."

Fourteen

"Well, what do you think?" asks Sabrina. I didn't hear her come outside.

I look over my shoulder and see her looking up at the sky like I had been.

"Well, it's definitely a maybe," I say.

Sabrina looks at me and stomps her foot. "Ga-abe, come on. Is it gonna snow or not?"

I laugh. "Seriously, it's maybe. I've been looking at the sky and checking the forecast on my computer. Nobody's saying for sure yet. But I think I might see some cirrostratus clouds."

Sabrina rolls her eyes and mouths "blah, blah, blah."

"Okay. Cirrostratus clouds usually mean rain or snow

will happen within twenty-four hours. But the problem is that they're so thin and so high they can be hard to see."

Sabrina frowns, but she's listening.

"You have to know what to look for. It's like a fuzzy halo around the sun. Or the moon if it's at night. What do you think? Do you see a halo?"

"You're supposed to be the angel, *Gabriel*. If anyone's going to see a halo, wouldn't it be you?"

I stick out my tongue and pretend to flap my wings. Sabrina giggles.

Sabrina looks up at the sky, closes one eye, then the other, opens both and shrugs. "A halo? I don't know. Maybe," she says.

"That's what I said. Maybe." We both laugh. Which doesn't really happen anymore. Not like it did before Sabrina started middle school and becoming popular became her mission.

"I guess sometimes it's good to be a weather dork, huh?" I say.

"Sometimes." Sabrina pulls the sleeves of her sweater down over her hands and hugs herself. "Well, even I can tell it's cold enough to snow. I'm going back inside. Let me know if anything changes. And let me know when Grandma and Grandpa get here."

It's Christmas Eve, and Sabrina and I are hoping for a white Christmas even though it almost never happens in our part of North Carolina. But it could happen. It really could.

We all spill out of my mom's cookie van—it's a regular minivan except for the giant cookie with a bite out of it and the words "Heavenly Bites" on either side.

The church bells are ringing. They're playing "Joy to the World" loud enough that I can feel each note in my chest. Midnight Mass is special. Even though we come here to this same church every Sunday, Midnight Mass still seems magical. Like anything could happen.

I stop for a minute to check the skies again. That haze around the moon could be from cirrostratus clouds. And if it is, that could mean snow is coming. So we could have a white Christmas. But that's a lot of coulds. A lot of coulds that add up to one big maybe.

"Gabe, come on." My dad's on the steps, holding the door open for other families as they go inside. He's waiting for me. I stop thinking about the snow, jog past the nativity scene—no baby Jesus yet—and climb the steps two at a time.

St. Jude Church has been here since the town started. It looks old, but in a good way. It feels old when you sit down and find actual grooves in the wood pews from all the butts that have sat there. Sometimes you get a groove that doesn't quite fit your own butt, and it can be hard to get comfortable. And it smells old—the wood, the candles and, even when it's not being used, the incense that always tickles my nose.

We walk inside, and there's my mom, standing in our usual pew and waving her entire arm to make sure we see her. Because my mom's in charge of all things Christmas, including getting us here, we're early. Being early and the fact that she's in the same pew we sit in every Sunday mean we can find her without the jumping and the waving. Beside me, my dad chuckles and waves back so she knows we see her. Thankfully, she stops and sits down.

I follow my dad and slide into the pew after him, on the end. Perfect. My dad won't notice if I fall asleep for a minute or if I'm not singing or whether or not I'm standing up straight. My mom notices all of that and more.

"Merry Christmas, Carpenters," says a voice from over my shoulder. I turn around. It's Mrs. Piccarelli. Mr. Piccarelli, Becca and all the boys make a wobbly line behind her.

"Merry Christmas, Gabe," whispers Becca.

I smile and grunt something that's supposed to be, "Merry Christmas."

Becca follows the rest of her family into the pew right across the aisle. She goes in last. So we're separated by seven feet of stone floor. I can almost pretend she's sitting next to me without the nausea I'd be feeling if she actually was that close.

After the choir sings what feels like every Christmas song there is, Mass begins. Stand up. Sit down. Stand up again. And then I start to feel a cramp in my eyes. I've been staring over at Becca while keeping my head pointed straight ahead. And my eyes have been making a hard right turn for so long that I think they might be stuck looking in that direction. Great. Like I need something else to go with my uneven arms and genius status to make me an even bigger freak.

I'm so busy thinking about my cramping eyes that at first I don't notice it. Then my nose starts to twitch. And the twitch turns into a tickle. It's Midnight Mass on Christmas Eve. And it's offertory time, which means incense. A lot of incense. The altar server hands the thurible to Father McSwain. And he starts to swing it. And the smell of incense is everywhere.

"Achoo! Achoo! Achoo!" I sneeze so many times I can't see. And they're not quiet sneezes. But everything else goes quiet. Father McSwain stops praying. The organist even stops playing. The only sound is my sneezes. Over and over, my sneezes.

When I'm finally done, my eyes are streaming with tears, and I can't see. I do the only thing I can think of. I sit down. But all of the sneezing must have knocked me sideways. Because the pew I was going to sit on isn't there, and I land on the stone floor in the middle of the aisle.

The unmistakable sound of a fart—blasting from my anal sphincter like a trumpet—shatters the silence, followed by the sounds of people trying not to laugh. Most don't try hard enough. There are snickers, chuckles, snorts, and a few flat out guffaws. And one quiet giggle that sounds like wind chimes. Becca's giggle. Becca is laughing at me.

My dad hauls me up by my armpits and drags me back into the pew.

"Are you all right?" The words are right, but the way he says it and the look on his face tell me something else. He's embarrassed. By me.

How could I possibly be all right? I just sneezed so hard I fell down and then farted in the middle of Midnight Mass.

I guess the rest of the Mass happened because suddenly, it's over. And everyone is wishing everyone else

"Merry Christmas." I just want to get out. I zig and zag around people, ignoring anyone who looks at me or tries to talk to me.

I figure they'll either try to make me feel better about what happened or make a joke about it. I'm not in the mood for either. Finally, I see the door straight ahead. I push through the last of the people ahead of me and I'm out.

It's snowing. It happened. While I was inside humiliating myself in front of hundreds of people, it was snowing. There's at least an inch on the ground, and it's still coming down. I can't believe it. All the coulds that needed to happen happened and turned the maybe into a yes. It's snowing.

An arm encircles my shoulders and squeezes tight. Without looking, I know it's my grandpa. And I know he won't say anything about what happened inside.

"Look at that," he says. "How about if you and I walk home?"

"Will Mom let us? It's really late."

"I already cleared it with her. Let's go."

We start walking down the sidewalk that will take us the five blocks to my house.

"Wait for me," yells Sabrina. I turn to see her careening down the sidewalk, slipping and sliding in her shoes that are not made for running in the snow.

Sabrina catches up to us, but before she can open her mouth to say anything, Grandpa says, "You can come with us if you promise not to say anything to Gabe about what happened."

Sabrina nods but looks at me and smirks.

"Not one word, Sabrina, or you go in the van with the others." Our grandpa is almost never stern, but there's no mistaking he's not kidding. I think Sabrina knows it, too. She presses her lips together and crosses her heart with her pink-mittened hand.

We walk home together, three across on the sidewalk. It's really late, it's really cold, and it's so still and quiet. When we talk, it's in whispers.

Walking up the driveway, I stop and look up at the falling snow, my mouth open in a huge yawn. Suddenly something cold and wet hits me in the face. It's a snowball. I look around and see my grandpa laughing, ready to launch another one at me.

"Snowball fight," he says, and this one hits me in the chest.

"You're on." I scoop up enough snow to pack into a pretty decent snowball. But instead of hitting my grandpa, it sails off and smacks Sabrina in the head. She comes after me and stuffs snow down the neck of my jacket, not bothering to make a snowball. I'm laughing so hard I can't stand up, but I manage to dump a handful of snow over her head.

Snow is flying all over the place, and Grandpa, Sabrina, and I are covered with it when the front door opens. It's my mom. And she's smiling. "Come inside—it's freezing. I've got hot chocolate waiting for you."

As we walk up the front steps, I ask Grandpa, "Are you sure you liked your gift?" My grandpa is weirdly hard to buy for, but I thought the journal to record seismic activity was pretty good.

"I loved my present. It's a great present. But you are my gift. You and Sabrina and this." Grandpa rubs one more handful of snow in my hair and says, "Merry Christmas, my Gabe."

I'm wet, I'm tired, and there's still the whole falling and farting in church thing, but I say, "Yep, Grandpa. Merry Christmas."

Fifteen

Eleven days of Christmas break sounded like a good thing. But Linc got dragged away on something called an "educational vacation" with his parents, so he's been gone the whole time. And Maya and I aren't friends anymore so I couldn't hang out with her either. So with only two days to go, this Christmas break is looking like it'll go down in Gabe Carpenter history as eleven days of boring.

The only good thing is that since I haven't had anything better to do, I've done tons of work on my Academic Olympics project. It's almost ready.

I grab my project notes and go in search of my dad. I found something interesting that I want to show him.

The sounds of a basketball game on TV are coming from the family room. That's where I find my dad, stretched out in his recliner, half asleep.

One of the Carolina U. players is at the foul line, waiting to take his shot. He bounces the ball a couple times, crosses himself, and shoots. He misses the shot.

"Come on," my dad yells and sits up in his chair. "You gotta make those."

"He should try shooting granny style," I say.

My dad looks at me and says, "What?" before turning back to the TV. The same guy misses another free throw.

"I'm doing research for my project—the science of sports—and it's true. He should try granny style—you know, underhand." I sit down in the chair next to my dad and pull out my research.

"Gabe, no one shoots granny style. It looks ridiculous."

"Yeah, but if it works, who cares? My research says that it can have a huge effect on free throw percentages. For everyone, but especially for taller players. It's all about the arc of the ball and backspin."

I can tell my dad's listening to me with about half an ear, but I keep going. "A long time ago, a player named Rick Barry shot his foul shots granny style, and his free throw percentage was like 90 percent. And Wilt Chamberlain only shot around 50 percent—he shot overhand. There's lots of science—physics—to support it."

My dad harrumphs. "I know who Rick Barry is. He played when I was a kid, not 'a long time ago.' And he looked ridiculous."

"Do you want to go try it?" I ask.

My dad looks back at the TV. His team just lost by two points. Those two missed free throws could have tied the game.

"All right." He gets up, stretches, and grabs my notebook, looking through my notes and muttering while he reads. "Come on. Let's see if your science holds up."

We put on coats and hats and lace up our shoes. I grab a couple basketballs from the hall closet, and we head outside.

"Okay, let's see this," says my dad.

I haven't tested my theory yet. I just have to hope the science is right—that this really does work.

I walk to the crack in the driveway that serves as our foul line and bounce the basketball a few times—woomp, woomp, woomp. I close my eyes and picture it going in, then bend over, swing the ball between my legs and throw it up underhand—granny style. It goes in!

"Hey, it works." I turn and grin at my dad. He's frowning and holding the ball.

"Try it again." My dad passes me the ball.

I do and it goes in—again. My smile gets bigger.

"You never make two shots in a row."

"I know." It's true. It almost never happens. "But see, it's the backspin. When the ball hits the backboard, it has a better chance of falling down into the net."

"I need more data." Now my dad is smiling.

I take ten shots and make six. That's at least three times as many as I'd ever make shooting overhand.

Finally, my dad decides to give it a try. He looks around like he's making sure none of the neighbors is watching. Then he bends over, and throws the ball up underhand. It goes in.

"See, granny style works," I say.

"Hold on. Let me try something," says my dad. "If we're talking science, we need to do an experiment. I'll take ten shots overhand and ten underhand. I'm not calling it granny style." He grins at me. "And we'll see."

"Okay. I'll keep track in my notebook."

My dad makes four out of ten overhand and eight out of ten granny style—I mean underhand.

"Wow." He says after his last granny style shot goes in. "That's pretty amazing."

Wow is what I'm thinking, too. But not about my dad's free throws. About us being out here playing basketball together. About him talking to me about science and sports. This is a first. And it's pretty cool.

"You should tell Ty about this," says my dad.

What?

"The team has been struggling from the line. They lost a close one last week against Overton Prep, and Ty missed four free throws late in the game."

"Really?" I say, even though I don't care.

"Yeah. You know, Gabe, you should invite Ty over, and we could play some ball."

And the good feeling I was having is gone. Playing with me isn't enough. He wants to play basketball with someone who's actually good at it.

My mom pokes her head out of the door before I have to think of something to say.

"Joe," she says. "Don't forget you need to pick Olivia up at 5:30 so we can leave here no later than 5:45."

"What's going on?" I ask. "Why is Olivia coming over?"

Olivia is Olivia Ling. Maya's sister. She's sixteen and a junior in high school.

I look at my mom. She smiles—too big.

"Tell me." I fold my arms across my chest and give my mom a look that she's used on me hundreds of times. Head cocked to the side and eyebrows up. It's the look she gives me when she wants the whole story. And that's what I want. The whole story.

"Well, you know Dad and I go to the New Year's Eve formal at church every year."

My mom's fidgeting with a stack of recipes she's holding. My mom doesn't fidget. Something's up.

"Yeah."

"Well, Dad and I talked about it, and we're not comfortable coming home so late and leaving you and Sabrina home alone, so—"

"Wait. Don't tell me you got us a babysitter. No way."

This cannot happen. Sure Olivia used to babysit for us. When I was ten. But I'm twelve—almost a teenager. And I'm in seventh grade. No one in seventh grade needs a babysitter.

"Now calm down," says my dad.

Yeah, that's not going to happen.

"Olivia's not going to babysit," says my mom. "I just asked her to come and keep you and Sabrina company. Sabrina's excited about it."

"Of course, Sabrina's excited. She thinks Olivia's her fairy godmother or her Yoda or something. Her roadmap to popularity."

"That's not very nice," says my mom.

"It wasn't supposed to be nice," I snap. "Are you paying

her? Are you paying Olivia to keep us company?"

"Yes, of course, I'm paying her."

"Newsflash, Mom. That's called babysitting. I can't believe you're doing this to me." I slam the basketball on the ground and stomp toward the front door.

"Don't forget to ask Ty if he wants to come over and shoot baskets with us sometime," my dad calls after me.

I spin around and glare at my dad, my hands at my sides in tight fists.

"Sure thing, Dad. Even though he's a jerk who thinks he's too cool to even talk to me, I'll make sure I ask him to come over and play with *you*."

My dad smiles like he thinks I'm kidding or something. He doesn't get it.

"Maybe then you could invite Ty to Thanksgiving dinner next year, and you could pick him for your team." My voice sounds strange. Being this mad is making it hard to get the words out.

"What?" my dad says. My mom gives him a look that must clue him in because then he says, "I thought you said you were okay that I picked Will."

"I lied."

I push past my mom into the house and speed toward my room.

"Gabe, wait—" my mom's voice follows me down the

hall. She probably says more, but I can't hear her because when I get to my room I slam the door.

The hand that I didn't use to slam my door is still clutching my notebook. All of the research I've done for my project is in here. But does it matter? For a minute, I thought my dad actually understood, but all he cares about is playing basketball with Ty. I know Maya doesn't care. She probably hopes I crash and burn.

All the excitement I had about my findings is gone, like it leaked out of me all over the driveway. I take the notebook and wing it across the room. It slides under my bed and smacks into the wall. I flop down on my bed and close my eyes.

Like a movie playing on the inside of my eyelids, I can see my dad laughing and shooting granny style free throws. Then I see him telling me to ask Ty to come over for a game. My eyes snap open to stop the movie. I punch my pillow and stuff it under my head. I tell myself I don't care what my dad thinks, which probably isn't true. I also tell myself that I don't care if we win, which probably is.

I wish I'd never left my room. And I might never leave again. I can't believe my dad is so clueless. And my mom got us a babysitter. Perfect. Happy Stinking New Year.

My parents yelled goodbye through my door a while ago, which means they're gone. If they're gone, that means Olivia is here. Sabrina's insane giggling is another clue that Olivia is here.

Olivia is kind of the anti-Maya. She's popular. But not regular popular. She's the girl that even the popular girls want to be like. And even though Maya's pretty, Olivia is seriously beautiful. Back when Maya was still my friend, I could get Linc to come with me to her house because he knew he might get to stare at Olivia. She's nice and funny, too—but that part is like Maya. Or like Maya used to be.

I don't want to leave my room. But I'm hungry. Really, really hungry. And now I smell pizza. It's like the aroma of hot, melty cheese and pepperoni is somehow snaking its way down the hall and under my door. I try not to think about it. I try to think about something else.

It's not working. The pizza is too powerful. The smell— it's overwhelming my brain. I can't think about anything but how much I want to bite into a big, melty, gooey, pepperoni filled slice. And then eat another one and another one until I can't eat anymore.

I look at my pen, then at the guys swimming around in their bowl. "You know, Superman was powerless against kryptonite. For me, I guess it's pizza. I'm going out there."

A glug so small I almost can't hear it is all I get back. For the first time in a long time, I wish I had a dog—at least a dog would pretend to listen.

I pull the door open and rush out thinking about one thing. Pizza. Then I'm falling. And landing—in something hot and slippery. I lift up one sore butt cheek and see why the smell of pizza seemed like it was coming from right outside my door.

Because it was.

Someone left a piece of pizza on a paper plate in front of my door. And I stepped in it—and fell.

"Gabe, are you okay?"

I look up and see Olivia coming down the hall, Sabrina following her like a puppy. Of course, Sabrina's laughing.

"I'm fine," I say. "Who put the pizza outside my door?"

"It was me," says Olivia. "I'm really sorry. I thought it would get you to come out of your room." She puts out her hand for mine. I let her pull me up.

"Well, it worked." I look at Olivia and smile. I can't help it. It's actually impossible not to smile at Olivia. She's looking at me with a worried line between her eyebrows and a little smile that doesn't show any teeth.

"Gabe, why don't you change your pants and then come have pizza with us?" says Olivia.

I start to shake my head, but she grabs my arm. "Please."

"Okay, I'll be there in a minute."

She gives me a look that, for a second, makes her look just like Maya. I push the feeling of missing Maya back down somewhere near my liver where I've been keeping it, go back in my room, and change into a cleanish pair of jeans from the floor in my closet.

When I walk into the kitchen, Sabrina's gabbing on the phone—probably with Becca. I head straight for the open pizza boxes on the counter and grab a slice. The first bite is like the answer to a prayer. It's gooey, it's melty, it's loaded with pepperoni. Ahhh.

Olivia puts a glass of sweet tea in front of me and says, "I told her she's being stupid."

I know she's talking about Maya, but I don't know what to say. So I don't say anything. I just keep chewing. Olivia doesn't seem to notice or care. She keeps talking.

"Maya's miserable without you. She's moping around and cranky all the time. So I told her she's stupid."

There's that word again.

"Maya's not stupid," I say.

"She's *being* stupid," says Olivia. "You don't throw

away real friends. You just don't. And she did. So she's stupid. That's what I told her."

I raise my eyebrows at her in a question.

Olivia laughs softly. "Yeah, she slammed her door in my face."

Sixteen

When the phone rings, I'm shoving half a piece of left-over pizza in my mouth with one hand and scratching my armpit with the other. After the fourth ring, I answer the phone with the armpit scratching hand and manage a garbled hello.

It's Mrs. Piccarelli. She's calling to tell me that she has my money for last week's tutoring session with Becca. I tell her I'll come pick it up in a little while.

I open my mouth and start shoveling in the rest of my breakfast. Chew, swallow, repeat until it's gone. Then down the hall to the bathroom. I look in the mirror and decide there's no way I can go over there looking like this. My bed head is legendary, and I'm wearing sweats with a mystery stain on one knee. So, I take a shower and get dressed, and I'm sort of ready. Sort of because what if Becca's home? What if she answers the door?

Linc's coming home today. He's going to want to know what happened while he was gone. And right now the answer to that is nothing. Linc keeps talking about action. He took action and wrote a really bad love poem and suddenly everyone thinks he's Romeo. He should have crashed hard, but he didn't. And he said it's because he took action. He said he felt like he could fly.

I can't stop thinking about the word "action" as I walk down the street thirteen houses and cross to the other side. I walk up the sidewalk, climb the steps to the front porch, and ring the doorbell. The door opens and there she is. Becca. Action.

So I open my mouth without knowing what's going to come out.

"Hey, Becca, I was wondering. Would you want to go see a movie with me next weekend?"

What's happening? It's like my mouth is moving on its own without my brain telling it what to do. The rest of my body is absolutely still with the shock of it, but not my mouth.

It's still going. "I can have my dad drive us. You can pick the movie. Friday or Saturday—it doesn't matter which."

And then panic washes over me like a wave. What just happened? Did I just ask Becca to go to the movies with me? Why did I do that? But I know why.

Action.

It takes a few seconds for my brain to join back up with the rest of my body. When it does, I notice that Becca hasn't said anything. I look at her, and she seems frozen. And I don't think it's because she's cold. She's not moving—her hand is still on the handle of the door from when she opened it. Her eyes are big and unblinking in her face, and the smile she gave me when she said "hi" is still there—stuck.

Becca finally shakes her head like she's waking herself up, frowns for a second, and then smiles again. But this smile is with just her mouth—no nose crinkle.

"Oh, like with you and Sabrina." She says the Sabrina part louder than the rest—like if she wrote it down, Sabrina's name would be in bold print or all capitals or something.

I start to explain that I didn't mean Sabrina, but Becca keeps talking. "Yeah, that'd be fun but not next weekend. I'm, um, busy next weekend. But here's the money my mom owes you, and thanks again for helping me. It's really cold so I'd better go. Bye." I stare and feel my mouth drop open. I didn't know a person could say that many words that fast without taking a breath. Becca steps back and closes the door quickly, but quietly.

I stand there for a minute with the money lying in my outstretched hand. I don't have any idea what just happened. Did I just get turned down? Maybe she didn't understand that I meant going to see a movie with just me, not me and Sabrina. Or maybe she did, and she was so disgusted by the thought that she made up the first thing that came to mind.

As I start walking home, I wait for the feeling Linc talked about. The feeling of almost being able to fly because I finally had the guts to take action. But as I trudge toward home, I stumble over an uneven spot in the sidewalk and barely keep myself from falling. Not flying—not even close to flying.

Linc's bike is on its side in my driveway. He's back. I listen for the sound of dribbling and, hearing none, go inside to look for him. I find him in the kitchen, straddling a chair backward—which my mom never lets me get away with. There's a plate of cookies in front of him.

"Hey, you're back."

"Yeah, I was just telling your mom about my trip. My parents dragged me to an opera. Can you believe it? It was in Italian. And my mom got mad when I fell asleep."

He takes a cookie and sticks the entire thing in his mouth. My mom just smiles at him. If I did that, she'd smack me.

"I'm going to my room," I say. "You can come or you can stay here and have some more girl talk with my mom."

I turn and start out of the kitchen. Then I change my mind and grab a cookie for myself—to eat in my room. My mom starts to say something, but then stops. She gives me one of those mom looks like she knows something's wrong. Then she taps one finger of her right hand on the top of her left hand three times—her secret code for "I love you." I pretend not to see.

Linc's a few steps behind me. He walks into my room, grabs a pillow off my bed, and slides down the wall until his butt hits the carpet. The pillow gets stuffed behind his head.

"Something happened," he says. "Obviously it's not something good because you're not even happy to see me." Linc gives me a cheesy smile. "And you should be. So start talking."

"I would be happy to see you if the not-good thing— which I think might be colossally not good—wasn't your fault." I lie face down on my bed and groan. I can't breathe very well, but I decide I don't care. I groan again.

"How can it be my fault? I just got home."

I pick my head up just long enough to say, "You told me to take action. You told me taking action made you feel like you could fly. You told me to woo. It's all your fault."

"Becca? You took action with Becca? What did you do? Tell me—what did you do?" Linc's voice keeps getting louder.

Before I can answer him, my bedroom door flies open. I turn my head and see Sabrina standing there. And there's crazy in her eyes.

"What were you thinking?" Sabrina yells. "Really, Gabe, what were you thinking? Did you seriously just ask my best friend to go to a movie with you? Did you ask Becca on a date? A date? Because that's what she said happened, but I can't believe you'd do that. So tell me, Genius, are you that stupid?"

"Whoa," says Linc. "You really did it. You took action." He whoops and slaps his hand on his leg. "What'd she say? Did she say yes?"

"What?" says Sabrina. She turns the crazy eyes toward Linc and then they come back my way. "Shut up, Linc. Gabe, you start talking. Tell me Becca was wrong. Tell me you're not that clueless—that you're not trying to ruin my life. Tell me. Did you ask Becca on a date?"

Sabrina's hands are bunched into fists at her sides, and I can tell she wants to hit me—or worse. I think about lying. Telling her that Becca misunderstood. But I'm so sick of her and Maya and my dad and everyone else who acts like there's something wrong with me. So I tell her the truth.

"Yes, I did. I asked Becca on a date. And I'm glad I did."

Linc starts to laugh. Then he falls sideways onto the floor and howls. Sabrina looks at me, then at Linc. She kicks Linc in the shin, gives me a look that will stay with me for a while, and runs out the door yelling for my mom.

Linc sits up, rubs his leg, and asks again, "What'd Becca say?"

I just shake my head no. "I don't know why I did it, Linc. It was like someone else took over my mouth and made me say it."

Linc grins at me. "I know. That's exactly what it's like. See, I've been doing all this research for my project and being in love or really in like makes you crazy. Isn't that great?"

"So, I'm crazy? And that's supposed to be great? What are you talking about?"

"When you like a girl like you like Becca, stuff happens in your brain—chemicals like dopamine and adrenaline are released and different parts of your brain are affected. It's awesome. It's not just your heart, it's in your brain, too."

"So you found out love or like or whatever can change your brain and make you act like you're crazy—like you're insane even? And you didn't tell me that?" This conversation is making me crazy. "You didn't think I might need to know that so I didn't go and do something stupid like I just did?"

Linc just grins at me again, and I think about kicking him myself.

Seventeen

I bang my head on my locker one, two, three times, and let it rest there. My locker won't open. Again. Did I think some miracle happened over Christmas break and I'd magically be able to open my locker like every other kid clomping up and down the halls carrying just one or two classes worth of books? Maybe.

"Need some help?" asks a voice from behind me. I pivot my head far enough to see that it's our school janitor, Mr. Simmons. He's holding a broom wide enough to sweep half the hallway at once and wearing a smirk on his face.

"Yes, I do need help. Like I've told you a hundred times, I can't open my locker. Every day it's the same thing.

I spin the stupid combination around, listen for the click, and then pull. And nothing. Every day. So yes, I do need help."

I know I'm ranting, but I can't help it. Because it's true—I've talked to Mr. Simmons about my locker lots of times.

"Relax, Genius. Let's see what the problem is," says Mr. Simmons. "Hold this."

Here comes Becca with Sabrina and their friend Hannah. I can tell the exact moment they see me standing there holding the enormous broom. Sabrina glowers at me, and Becca's eyes land on me and then dart away. Hannah just looks at me and giggles. Then she whispers something in Becca's ear, and they both giggle.

I want to say something. I want to shout that I only did what I did because apparently I was crazy, and my brain went haywire. But it's back to sort of normal, and now I wish I'd never asked Becca to go to the movies. Of course, I don't say any of that. I just stand there and listen to them giggling.

"Tell me the combination again," says Mr. Simmons.

I turn away from Becca's giggles and Sabrina's scowl. "34 right, 4 left, 16 right." I sigh hugely and wait for the inevitable. The same thing that happens every time. And, there it is. My locker door pops open almost happily.

Mr. Simmons turns around and smirks at me again. "I can't fix it if it's not broken." He slams my locker door shut, grabs his broom and walks away. I watch his shoulders move up and down as he laughs.

I glare at my locker, my stupid unopenable—by me anyway—locker and turn toward my first class, dragging my backpack behind me with my right arm. I don't care anymore if my right arm gets stretched out until I can scratch my ankle without bending over. Because really, how much worse could that make things? Everyone already thinks I'm a freak, my second-best friend isn't my second-best friend anymore, and I totally humiliated myself with Becca.

I stop in front of the Saint Jude statue and glare at him, too. When I take a step into the nook, I almost get knocked down by Ty Easterbrook coming out. Before I can wonder what he was talking to Saint Jude about, Ty steps on my foot and shoves past me without saying anything. There's a good chance he actually flattened my foot.

I crouch down like I need to tie my shoe. Instead I check for broken toes and whisper, "Really? Could you help a guy out once in a while? If I'm not a lost cause right now, who is?" I look up. Nothing. Not even a twitch. No sign that he hears me. It looks like I'm on my own.

When I walk into G.A.S. class, the first thing I see is Maya and Cameron whispering and laughing with their heads close together. I stop and stare at the weirdness. Maya and Cameron are not friends. I don't know for sure since she doesn't talk to me anymore, but I'm pretty sure Maya thinks he's a moron. And now she's whispering in his ear and giggling. Giggling.

They turn and see me standing there. Maya elbows Cameron in the arm, and they start laughing again, but louder. And I don't have to be a genius to know that whatever they're laughing about has something to do with me. For some reason, I just stand there and wait to find out what's going to happen next.

Cameron stands up, looks around, and makes sure everyone is watching him. Then he says, "So, Gabe, did your babysitter tuck you in and read you a bedtime story?"

I look at Maya. She looks right back at me—something in her face reminds me of how Sabrina looked at me in the hall this morning. Does Maya hate me, too? She must. Why else would she tell Cameron about Olivia being at my house on New Year's Eve?

"Cameron, that's enough. Please sit down," says Sister Stevie.

Cameron doesn't move.

Neither do I. I just stand there and don't say anything. Again.

But Cameron does. "It's sweet that your mommy thinks you still need a babysitter. Is it because you're afraid of the dark? That would be ironic, don't you think? A supposed genius who's afraid of the dark and is too scared to stay home by himself."

Cameron looks up at the ceiling and laughs. He laughs and laughs. He bends over at the waist and laughs. Ty is laughing, too, and even Rachel giggles a little. Linc just sits at his desk, not laughing but not helping me either. And then there's Maya. She's standing next to Cameron, arms folded in front of her and smiling a smile that's more like a sneer.

Maya. Standing with Cameron. Making fun of me.

All of a sudden all the horrible feelings I've been having rush through me at once. All the rotten stuff that's happened that I've done nothing about. Said nothing about. And before I tell it to, my arm is moving forward—toward Cameron. And my hand is a fist, and the fist slams into Cameron's stomach. Hard.

Oooff.

That's the sound that Cameron makes at the same time he doubles over. Before I can tell it not to, my arm rears back and comes forward again.

Crack.

That's the sound my fist makes when it meets his nose.

"Gabe! Stop it—Gabe!"

That's Sister Stevie. Her voice sounds like it's coming to me through water. I can hardly hear her, and it doesn't matter what she's saying. I'm taking action.

Cameron stands back up, reaches out, and pushes me in the chest. He knocks me back and off balance a little bit. I don't care. Whatever this feeling is that's moving through me doesn't care. It just takes my arm back to hit him again. But someone grabs my other arm and pulls me to the side. There's no way I can stop my fist—it's moving forward too fast. And it runs into something that's not Cameron. It's Maya. It's Maya's face. I just punched Maya in the face.

Maya crumples to the floor, holding her hand over her left eye. And the whole world slows back down. I took action. And ended up punching Maya, a girl and my used to be second-best friend, in the face.

Eighteen

Cameron, Maya, and I sit on the wooden bench outside Mr. Dooley's office. It's long enough that no one has to sit next to anyone else, and hard enough to make it impossible to get comfortable.

I flex and unflex my hand while staring at my knuckles, which are bright red and hurt like crazy. I've never actually punched someone before. Now I've punched two people. And one of them was Maya.

I can't believe I punched Maya. I sneak a look at her out of the corner of my eye. She's sitting with her knees tucked up under her chin, holding an icepack on her eye. She hasn't moved since we got here and just stares straight ahead—melting water from the icepack dripping down and making a plopping sound as it hits the bench.

I want to say something. But what? I'm sorry I accidentally punched you? I'm sorry that you hate me? I'm sorry that you're so mad at me that you teamed up with a jerk and tried to make me look stupid? I'm sorry that it worked?

I should be sorry that I hurt Maya, and I am. I'm so sorry about that. But the rest of it—I'm not sorry. I took action. And I felt something—nothing like flying. But something.

"In my office—all three of you. Now."

It's Mr. Dooley, and if the vein throbbing in the middle of his forehead and the sweat on his lip mean what I think they mean, he's mad. Really mad.

I stand up and shuffle into the office behind Cameron and Maya. There are only two chairs other than Mr. Dooley's, so I pick the one empty spot on the wall to lean against and embark on an in-depth study of the toes of my shoes.

Mr. Dooley's breathing is loud in the silence of his office—he sounds like the horse I rode when we visited my mom's cousins in the mountains. I remember how the horse's nostrils flared, and I peek to see if Mr. Dooley's are doing the same thing. They are. And then I remember how that horse kicked me when I walked behind it.

"Someone better tell me what happened—and why—right now," says Mr. Dooley.

Silence.

I'm not saying anything. I'm done taking action for today. Cameron keeps poking at his nose with a tissue even though not one drop of blood has come out. Maya's still holding the dripping ice pack and staring into space.

"Okay, here's what I do know. I know that three of my brightest students—three members of my Academic Olympics team, including both team captains—got into a fight. A fistfight in Sister Stevie's class. And I was told that Gabe threw the first punch. But I can't believe that could be true. So I'm asking again. What happened?"

Dab, dab, dab. Cameron is still trying to drum up some evidence of an injury. He sits up straighter and opens his mouth. "That's right, Mr. Dooley. Gabe hit me. For no reason." Cameron turns and glares at me.

"No reason? Gabe Carpenter just hit you for no reason—is that what you're telling me Cameron?"

Cameron nods. "Yep."

"Maya? Do you have anything to say?"

Maya just shakes her head, flinging drops of water onto a stack of papers on Mr. Dooley's desk.

"Gabe? I was hoping to get your side of the story," says

Mr. Dooley. "Sister Stevie seemed to think that Cameron baited you. Is that true?"

I don't want to tell Mr. Dooley that Cameron was making fun of me because Maya's sister babysat for me. I don't want to say anything. So I don't.

Mr. Dooley sits and looks at me—the vein is pulsing faster and faster, and the sweat beads above his lip are getting bigger. He reaches his hand up to scratch his head, and I see today's pit sweat circles reach halfway to his belt. Mr. Dooley isn't having a good day either.

"If no one's going to tell me what really happened, then go back out in the hall and wait for your parents. Mrs. Francisco is calling them to come pick you up right now."

Mr. Dooley stands up, climbs over three piles of books and folders, and opens the door.

"You're all excused for the rest of the day. I'll speak with your parents when they arrive and let them know when you may return."

He's staring at me. It feels like the pulsing vein is talking to me, asking me what happened. I'm not talking to Mr. Dooley or his vein.

We take the same spots on the bench. No one talks.

I hear Mrs. Ling before I see her. She works at a bookstore around the corner from school, so I'm not surprised she got here this fast.

"Maya—what in the world? Are you all right?"

Mrs. Ling crouches in front of Maya, takes the icepack away, and cradles her face in her hands. She murmurs to Maya in Spanish and then kisses her cheek.

Then Mrs. Ling comes over to stand in front of me. "Gabe?"

I look up at her and say the first thing I've said since my fist ran into Maya's face. "It was an accident. I didn't mean it. It was an accident—I swear. I didn't mean to hurt her. I'd never hurt her."

Mrs. Ling, the mom of my former second-best friend, has always been like an extra mom for me. She looks me in the eye and says, "I believe you."

She ruffles my horrible hair and then lets her hand rest there for a minute. I swallow hard and bite the inside of my cheek to keep from crying.

Maya still hasn't looked at me or said anything. She and her mom walk into Mr. Dooley's office and then back out after a few minutes. Mrs. Ling is smiling so I guess Maya's not going to pay for this. But I bet I will.

I start counting by thirteens to pass the time until my mom comes. I get to 312 at the same time Cameron's parents—both of them—walk in. His mom is round all over and has even more freckles than Cameron does. She grabs him by the arm and hauls him up from the bench. His dad doesn't look at him at all. He just opens the door to Mr. Dooley's office without knocking. There's yelling, but I can't make out any of the words. The yelling stops, the door opens again, and Cameron and his parents come out. This time, Cameron's dad has him by the arm. It looks like Cameron will pay for this, too.

I've counted the number of pen and pencil marks on the wall—sixty-four—and the dead bugs in the ceiling light—twenty-three—and my mom still isn't here. This is weird. My mom should have been here by now. It's Monday, which is the day she spends doing paperwork at home. And our house is only six blocks away. She should have been here.

Mrs. Francisco walks by me and goes into Mr. Dooley's office. A few minutes go by and then she walks out and goes back to her desk, dabbing at her eyes with her finger. Did Mr. Dooley do something to make her cry?

Mr. Dooley pokes his head out of his office and says, "Gabe, your mom just called. I talked to her, and you are to walk home. Straight home. Your parents will meet you there."

There's something weird about the way he says this and something weird about the way he won't look at me. But getting out of here right now sounds good. Nothing has gone right here today.

Possible explanations and excuses fill my head as I walk home. I consider each one before deciding it won't work. What can I say to my parents that will make what happened today okay? The answer is—nothing. There's nothing I can say. I've never been in a fight at school. No notes, phone calls, or emails have ever come from teachers about my behavior. Never. So how can I explain that the first time I get in trouble it's for getting into a fight and punching a girl?

My feet bring me to the front porch before my brain comes up with anything for my mouth to say. I open the door, drag me and my backpack inside, take my shoes off, and put them in the basket. Nothing left to do but go find my mom.

A sniffling sound makes me look to the left. My parents are in the living room, sitting on the couch. And they're looking at me. I get a weird *déjà vu* kind of feeling.

The last time I came home from school and my parents were sitting on the living room couch looking at me, they told me I was a genius. For a split second, I think maybe they're going to tell me it was all a mistake and I'm the same Gabe I always was.

The knuckles on my left hand start to throb, reminding me that my parents probably want to talk about something other than whether or not I'm a genius.

"Gabe, come sit down. We need to talk to you," says my dad. He sounds so serious, not like my dad at all.

"I know I screwed up bad. I'm sorry. Really sorry. It's just—Cameron is such a jerk. Which I know isn't a reason to punch a person. And Maya—well, that was an accident. You have to believe me. I didn't mean to hit her—I would never hit her even though she started the whole thing."

I can't seem to stop the words that are coming out of my mouth even though I can hear myself and know that I'm not making any sense. And I can't seem to move from the doorway either. I don't want to come any closer to their disappointment. My mom even looks like she's been crying. She's clutching a crumpled tissue in her hand.

"Gabe, sit down," says my dad again. "Please." Something in his voice makes my radar go up. Something's going on. Something other than me getting into a fight.

I shuffle over to the chair and sit down on the edge. For some reason I can't explain, I want to stop time. I'm afraid to hear what's about to be said.

"What's wrong?"

Because something is wrong, isn't it? I don't think my mom's crying because I got in a fight.

"Honey, something happened," says my mom. "It's Grandpa."

The air goes out of my lungs, and I can't feel my body.

"What do you mean?" I ask. My voice sounds too loud in the room, and it cracks at the end of the question that I suddenly don't want anyone to answer. "What happened?"

"Grandpa had a heart attack," says my dad. "This morning while he was having breakfast with Grandma."

My dad won't look at me. It's like he's talking to the picture on the wall above my head. Why won't he look at me?

"But he's okay, right?"

No one answers me.

I jump up and stand so straight and so still. "Right? He's okay?"

My mom puts her head in her hands and starts to cry.

"Please. Please. Please." It's all I can think. All I can say, even though it comes out as the softest whisper. It's a prayer I'm praying with my whole self. Please, God.

When my dad finally looks at me, he shakes his head. "No, Gabe, he's not okay. I'm so sorry."

He's sorry? Sorry? That's what people say when

someone dies, and my grandpa cannot have died. That can't be what happened.

"He's gone, honey," says my mom. She stands up and comes to try and hug me.

I put my hands out to stop her. I don't think I could stand it if anyone touched me right now. I'm pretty sure I'd shatter into a million pieces. I know that's not scientifically possible, but I'm pretty sure that's what would happen.

I can't stay in this room. In this room where nothing ever happens, where no one ever goes. This room where they just told me my grandpa is dead. My grandpa. I can't stay here. I spin around and run to my bedroom, slamming the door and throwing myself face down on my bed.

Tears flow out of me like water from a faucet when you turn it on full blast. And the thought that keeps running through my head like it's on a loop is that I when I left school a little while ago, I didn't think my day could get any worse. How could I have been so wrong?

Nineteen

My nose tells me my grandma's coming before I see or hear her. My grandma smells like nobody else. It's a mix of perfume that smells like oranges and sports cream that smells like, well, sports cream. I guess she's still running. Even though.

She sits down next to me on the swing and lays my grandpa's briefcase in my lap. The briefcase he took with him everywhere.

"This is for you, honey. I want you to have it. Grandpa would want you to have it."

I run my hand over the leather. It's soft and worn, and there are scratches and marks on it from all of its adventures. And embossed on the front are his initials—W.J.C.

My grandpa's name was William, my middle name.

"I promise I'll take good care of it. But are you sure?"

"Well, I wanted to give you the motorcycle, but your mom said no." My grandma rolls her eyes.

A laugh spurts out of me before I can stop it. I clap my hand over my mouth and say, "I'm sorry."

"Nothing to be sorry about. Grandpa loved to laugh. He made me laugh every day."

I push off, and we move back and forth, back and forth. It's almost hypnotizing. I try to forget where I am and why I'm here. It doesn't work. Nothing works. Not even the clouds—cirrocumulus today—help. They do tell me why my hands and feet feel like popsicles. They're cold-weather clouds.

We're swinging in the backyard of my grandparents' house. Everyone else is inside for the reception after my grandpa's funeral. The house is full of people eating sandwiches without crusts and miniature cakes. It's like some kind of creepy party where everyone eats tiny food and talks quietly and looks guilty if they forget and laugh about something. Ugh.

So here I am, outside freezing my butt off and trying not to think too hard about what today means.

"You know how proud Grandpa was of you," says my grandma.

I nod and look down at my hands—they're clenched together in my lap. All day everyone has been telling me how proud my grandpa was of me. And I know it's true. But what I don't know is, did I deserve it?

"Gabe, look at me." I do. She looks so sad. Which is a stupid thing to think, because of course she's sad.

"I miss him already," I say.

It's true. Any time we had family stuff, I always hung out with Grandpa. A couple times today I caught myself looking for him. And then I'd remember.

"Me too, sweetie." She lays her head on my shoulder for a minute. My grandma, who runs marathons and is never still, rests there on my shoulder.

"He'd want me to tell you how much he loved you—loves you still. And how proud he is. Really and truly proud."

My grandma pulls something out of her pocket and hands it to me. It's a medal. I turn it over and read the name on the back. Saint Gabriel.

"I gave this to Grandpa the day you were born." She fiddles with the chain. "He wasn't a jewelry person so he never wore it around his neck, but he always had it with him."

"Really? I've never seen it before."

"He always had it with him," she repeats. "When you

were born, Gabe, he just knew. It's not that he didn't love the other kids, he did. He does. But there was always a special part of his heart just for you."

The medal feels warm in my hand. I slip the chain over my head and slide the medal under my shirt. It feels right.

"Thanks, Grandma. I'll keep it with me always."

She sits up and grabs my hand and kisses the knuckles that are still bruised.

"You're like him in so many ways," says my grandma.

"What do you mean? I'm not like him. I mean other than the hair." I run my fingers through it so it'll stand up straight. My grandma chuckles and pats it back down. "Grandpa was so smart and brave and . . . everything. He was an adventurer."

"Yes, he was all of those things. But so are you. He believed in you, Gabe. Always." She stands up and kisses me on the top of my head. "And so do I."

I watch my grandma walk back toward the house, her steps a lot slower than usual. Just before she gets to the door she turns back around. "You know, there's someone else who believes in you, too. Your dad."

I shake my head. "My dad just wishes I was good at sports. It's not like it was with Grandpa and me. It's not."

My grandma sighs and then says, "You know your dad never thought that Grandpa understood him. He was wrong, too." She squares her shoulders, opens the door, and goes back into the house full of sad people.

I didn't want to tell my grandma she's wrong. Not today, anyway. But my dad doesn't understand me at all. Maybe if I was good at basketball—or baseball or soccer or football or anything other than science and math— he'd try. Most of the time it seems like we don't speak the same language. But Grandpa and I did. I push off with my foot and set the swing back in motion. Back and forth, back and forth.

Twenty

Every stone I try to skip turns into a plunk. I hear my grandpa's voice in my head telling me to get my arm in position and to flick my wrist sharply. But still, plunk.

I haven't been thinking about school or the Academic Olympics or the fight or what's going to happen tomorrow. My grandpa dying wiped all of that from my brain. But I have to go back to school in the morning, and I'm sure everyone knows what happened. All of it.

And now I can't stop thinking. It seems like everything has been upside down since I found out about being a genius. This whole time it has felt like everyone else was deciding what me being a genius was supposed to mean. The problem is that I don't know what it means for me. If it even matters to me.

Because a lot of stuff didn't change. A lot of stuff is still really hard. Like girls, and making a shot outside three-point range—or inside three-point range—and opening my stupid locker.

My grandpa told me to be proud of my brain, to have faith in my ability and treat it with respect. But what does that mean, and how do I do it?

I feel around on the ground until I find a perfect stone for skipping. It's flat and smooth and big enough without being too big. I feel the stone's weight in my hand, flip it around a few times until it feels right, take my arm back and flick. Skip, skip, skip, skip, skip, skip, skip, skip, skip, skip, skip, and sink. Eleven skips. Eleven! That's my all-time high.

In the middle of my celebratory fist thump, I hear the faint squeak of bicycle brakes and then footsteps crunching through the brush. I take a peek over my shoulder and see Maya walking toward me. I turn back and look at the creek. I'm not really surprised to see her. The only surprising thing is how not surprised I am.

"Hey," she says in an un-Maya-like small voice. "Can I sit?"

I shrug.

She sits next to me, criss-cross applesauce style like she's in first grade. Maya blows her bangs up out of her eyes and that's when I see it. She has a black eye. Well, black eye isn't right because it's not black. It's yellow and green and blue with a few spots of purple. I did that. And even though I'm really mad at Maya for everything she did, I feel sick to my stomach when I see it.

"Sorry about your eye."

"It's okay. It was an accident." Maya gathers stones and dead leaves into a pile in front of her legs. "Also, I kind of deserved it."

Now I am surprised. Maya never admits when she's wrong. Never.

I open my mouth to tell her it's okay. Then I close it. Because it's not. None of it.

"Yeah, you kind of did," I say.

Maya sits up straight and whips her head to look at me. I guess she wasn't expecting me to say that either. Her eyebrows are high in her forehead. But she doesn't say anything. She just goes back to gathering stones and leaves. I go back to staring at the creek.

"Sorry about your grandpa." She and her mom were at the funeral Mass. I saw them but didn't talk to them. I didn't talk to anyone really.

"Thanks."

"I know how much he . . . I mean he was just so. . . ."

"Yeah, I know."

She keeps making her pile and I keep skipping stones—none of them go more than two or three skips because I'm not really trying. I just need something to do with my hands.

"My grandpa is kind of the reason that I need to tell you something," I say. I feel for his medal through my sweatshirt. "I am sorry for hitting you. But I'm not sorry for anything else."

"Anything else?"

"I'm not sorry that I'm a genius and it makes you mad. I'm not sorry that me getting a higher score on some IQ test made you feel bad about you. Because I didn't do anything. You did. You decided to stop being friends over something so stupid. You decided to treat me like dirt and humiliate me. You did all that." I stop talking to breathe. Because I hadn't been.

"You're right," says Maya. "About all of it." She's talking to the pile.

"I know I am. And you should know that I've decided some things." I don't tell her that I decided it just now. "I'm not going to be embarrassed about being a genius. And I'm not going to pretend that you're smarter than me just to make you feel better. Because you're smarter in some ways, and I'm smarter in others. But does that really matter?"

"No, none of it matters." There's a hitch in Maya's voice that says she's trying not to cry. "I was a jerk, okay? Is that what you want me to say? I was a jerk."

"Yeah, I guess that is what I want you to say." I reach over and poke Maya in the arm—not hard, but enough to knock her off balance a bit. She looks over at me and smiles the tiniest smile. A smile so tiny you'd have to really know her face to see it. And I do. I smile back—big.

"Okay, so you're a genius, and I'm a jerk. But are we okay? Can we be okay again?" Maya tucks her hair behind her ear, and there's the black eye again.

"I think so. But I have one last question." Maya's eyebrow—the left one—goes up. "What was your poem about? The Mandarin haiku."

Maya takes a stone, holds it in her hand for a long time, and then skips it. It skips two times and then sinks. Even when I first taught her, she never had only two skips. She stares at the spot where her stone sank.

"You. It was about you. My best friend."

That was the last thing I was expecting her to say. And it makes everything okay. Because it means that even when she was being such a huge jerk to me, underneath it all she was still my friend.

"We're okay again." I look over at her and smile. "Now, what are we going to do to win this competition? Because I want to win."

"You do? I didn't think you cared about winning," says Maya.

"I do now."

We talk strategy until our toes start to freeze, and it's almost dark. I help Maya up, and we walk over to our bikes. I climb on mine, and I'm fastening my helmet when Maya looks over at me.

"You know, I kind of hated it when I heard that you asked Becca out."

What? What does that mean?

Maya just waves and rides away. "See you tomorrow."

Twenty-one

I turn the corner on the way to Sister Stevie's classroom and find Maya waiting for me in the hall. It seems like a long time since Maya waited for me for anything. But there she is.

"Hey," she says. "I thought it might make it easier if we walked in together. Since it's your first day back and Cameron's, too."

"Thanks."

Cameron. I guess I forgot to think about him. Cameron who I punched and who got suspended from school for three days just like I did. Cameron who loves trying to make me look stupid—and who's good at it.

Maya and I walk in together. Cameron is already there,

sitting at his desk with his head hanging down. I walk over and stand in front of him. Sister Stevie pops up from her desk chair and starts walking our way.

"I'm sorry I hit you," I say. "You were being a total creep to me, but I shouldn't have hit you. So, I'm sorry."

He looks up at me, stares for a minute with a totally blank look on his face, then cracks a smile. "You're right, I was a creep. It was just so easy. I kept waiting for you to do something to get me to stop, and you never did." He runs his finger down his nose. "And then you did. I was kind of impressed."

"Still, I'm sorry." I turn and look at Sister Stevie. "I'm sorry, Sister Stevie. Really."

"I know," she says. "And I'm sorry, too. Truly sorry— about your grandpa."

"Thanks," I say. Which is all I say to anyone who tells me they're sorry about my grandpa. Because I can't talk about it. I can hardly even think about it. So I just keep thinking about how to make sure he'll stay proud of me. Maybe this class and the competition can be part of it.

Maya is still standing next to me, our shoulders almost touching. Everyone else is in their seats.

I take a deep breath. "So, now that we're all here— let's figure out how we're going to win this competition. We've only got two weeks to get ready."

Sister Stevie smiles—the dimply smile from before the fight is back. "Gabe's right. We've got work to do. Let's hear where everyone is. Ty, how about you? How are things at the race track?"

Ty squirms around in his seat for a minute and then grabs a rolled-up paper that's sticking out of his back-pack. It looks like a poster. He unrolls it and just sits there for a minute. Then Ty starts talking—fast.

"I'm going to do this bigger for the competition—like an actual panorama of a racetrack. And these are equations and facts at specific points on the track where a property of physics is important to the car's or track's performance. And there'll be a 3-D model of a driver—I'll have anatomy and biology stuff about him. And . . ." Ty trails off.

"What?" he says. "Why is everyone staring at me? Is it a bad idea or something?"

"No," says Maya. "It's a great idea. Just a little surprising." It's such a perfectly Maya thing to say that I have to choke back a laugh.

Ty's face splotches a funny kind of red, and he grips the poster hard enough to wrinkle one side. "Are you saying you thought I wasn't smart enough to do something like this?"

"Nope. Just too cool for the rest of us." Maya and Ty have a stare down for a minute. Maya wins.

Ty chuckles. "That's fair. Okay. The basketball team lost a big game to Overton Prep last week. And I'm sick of losing to those Neanderthals. I want to win this. So let's win."

"Winning sounds good," says Maya. "Don't you think so, Gabe?"

"Absolutely. Winning sounds great." I grin at Maya. "How about everyone else? Where are you with your projects?"

Sister Stevie stands up and tosses her bouncy ball into the corner. She sits down behind her desk and takes out a book. "It looks like my captains have this under control. Let me know if you need me." She has a look on her face—like a secret smile—that reminds me of a look my mom gets when things turn out the way she wanted them to.

"Linc, where are you with your stuff?" asks Maya.

"It's under control." Linc's staring up at the ceiling, and he's slouched down so far in his chair that one nudge could send him crashing to the floor.

"Details, please," says Maya.

"Nope." Linc glances at Maya just long enough to make sure she's looking at him and then goes back to his ceiling examination. Maya sends me a look that means I'm in charge of Linc. Great. I already asked him, and he won't tell me anything either.

Everyone else seems like they're on track. By the end of class, we've got a plan.

I'm putting my notebooks and pens back in my backpack when I notice Ty standing in front of my desk, staring at the floor and chewing his lip.

"Um, is there anything in your research that could help me with my free throws?" he asks. "Coach is on me about it after the last game."

I wait a few beats. He finally meets my eyes, and I see he's serious. Ty Easterbrook wants my help. With sports.

"Yeah, sure," I say. "Shoot them underhand—granny style."

Ty looks like he wants to punch me. "That's not funny, Gabe."

"No, I'm serious. Here, I'll show you. It's physics—the arc and spin of the ball."

I take Ty through the information just like I did my dad. He nods a lot and asks a few questions.

Ty studies me for a long minute and then says, "But I'd look stupid."

I shrug. "Maybe. But if it works, who cares?"

More lip chewing and ground staring. "Uh, would you show me? Like maybe after school?"

"I guess so."

"Your house okay?" Ty asks.

"Sure." Keeping my answers as short as possible seems like a good idea since I'm still mostly convinced this is some kind of joke.

"Okay. I'll see you after school." Ty's halfway to the door when he glances back over his shoulder. "And thanks."

Maybe not a joke after all.

"Gabe?"

Sister Stevie says my voice in a way that makes me think she's said it more than once. Only then do I realize I haven't moved. Class has been over for a while, but I'm still sitting at my desk.

I look up at Sister Stevie, and all of a sudden I know I'm going to cry. I didn't know it five seconds ago, but I know it now. I can see by the way her face goes all soft and sad-looking that she knows it, too.

"Oh, Gabe. I know death can seem so unfair. So hard to understand," says Sister Stevie.

"Yeah." I take a deep breath and try to ignore the fact that it hitches a few times going in and coming back out. "But that's not really the thing."

"What is the thing?" Sister slides into Linc's chair and

turns toward me. As usual, her veil sits the slightest bit crooked on her hair. It almost makes me smile.

"I get that people die. I mean I hate that my grandpa did, but I get that it happens. Everyone dies, right?" I don't wait for an answer. "And I believe he's in heaven. 'Cuz that's where a person like my grandpa belongs. But the thing is, he didn't get to say goodbye."

Sister Stevie just looks at me, waiting. I guess she knows there's more I want to say and that I need a minute to figure out how to say it. I start talking, but softly so that if it doesn't come out just right, she won't notice.

"See, my grandpa would totally have wanted to say goodbye. He would have wanted to tell each of us he loved us and all kinds of things. He was like that. Always telling you stuff. Important stuff. I keep wondering what he would've said to me. And what I would've said back." My voice gets quieter still. "If I would've gotten it right."

Sister reaches over and puts her hand over mine. She's quiet for a minute, but I can tell she's praying because her lips are moving. Then she squeezes my hand, almost as hard as my grandma would. "Something tells me you would've gotten it exactly right."

I look out the window, craning my neck so I can see that sliver of sky. And there it is. The heaven sky. Altostratus clouds with a few rays of sun shining through, reaching down toward earth. Toward me. "He knows, doesn't he?"

"Yep. He knows." Sister Stevie smiles and stands up. She grabs a notepad from her desk and scribbles something on it. "A late pass for your next class."

I didn't even hear the bell, but it must've rung a while ago. I grab my stuff and head for the door, pulling my backpack behind me. Without turning around, I say, "Thanks, Sister. I'm going to make him proud. And you, too."

I don't stick around long enough to hear her answer.

Twenty-two

Swish. Swish. Swish. And again, swish.

Ty makes basket after basket—jump shots, three-point shots, even something really close to a dunk—while I think about the total weirdness of this situation. It's like I'm in a parallel universe or alternate reality or some other name for something that would never happen in the real world. Because Ty Easterbrook, star leading scorer of the St. Jude basketball team, should not be at my house looking for help with basketball. From me.

After he makes the millionth shot in a row, Ty dribbles over to where I sit leaning against the garage door. "So were you serious about this granny style free throw thing?"

"There's a lot of research to back it up."

"Show me. Before I try it, I want to see the research."

I was expecting this. Ty's not just a basketball star. Even if he doesn't want anybody to know, he's also a really smart guy who can take in and spit out facts as easily as he can make a lay-up.

"It's all in here." I hold out my notebook. Ty takes it and sits down next to me. For the next few minutes, the only noise is the sound of pages being turned. When he gets to the end, he hands the notebook back to me and stands up.

"Well, obviously all of your science is solid. It all makes sense on paper. But I want to see if it really works." Then he throws the basketball to me. "You first."

I measure fifteen feet out from the basket and draw a free-throw line with a stub of chalk. Two dribbles, then I grab the ball with both hands, bend at the waist, and throw it up, just like I showed my dad. And just like when I showed my dad, it goes in. Swish.

I get the ball and pass it to Ty. He stands on the line and dribbles a lot more than two times. When he finally stops, he mimics my moves, bending at the waist—stiffly— and throws the ball toward the net, underhand. Swish.

"Again." Ty takes the ball and takes another shot. Another swish. And another. And another.

After the fifth free throw in a row goes in, Ty stops. "Can I ask you something?"

"Sure." I figure it's something about my research.

"What were you talking to Saint Jude about?"

"What?"

"The day I saw you in there. And stomped on your foot. Sorry about that, by the way. I was asking for help with this—with my free throws. But what were you asking about?"

"Pretty much everything but free throws." The truth falls out of my mouth before I can stop it.

Ty sends a bounce pass my way, and I actually catch it. "Wanna see who gets to ten first?"

"Granny style?"

"Let's call it underhand, okay?"

I take the ball and line up, ready for my first shot. Swish.

I'm still replaying it in my head as I walk to my locker. Me, Gabe Carpenter, beating Ty Easterbrook at a free-throw competition.

34 right, 4 left, 16 right. Listen for the click and lift.

It opened. It actually opened. I blink twice to make sure I'm really looking at the inside of my locker. I am.

There's not much in there since I've only had it open two other times this year, but there's my favorite gray sweatshirt and something that smells like an old lunch. It's my locker. And I opened it.

"Whoa," says a voice from behind me. "Did you do that?"

It's Linc, standing there with his arms folded around the one notebook he's carrying.

"Yep." I can't stop the grin that spreads across my face. "Let's go." I grab my notebook, history book, and Superman pen and head to class with Linc, pulling nothing behind me. Just walking to class like everyone else.

On the way past, I pause for a second and salute Saint Jude. I telepathically tell him I'm sorry for being mad at him. I get it now. He didn't help me because I never was a lost cause.

Twenty-three

My mom drops us off in front of the Central Carolina College science building. There's a big sign that says "Welcome Olympians" on the lawn. Being called an Olympian makes me feel like I should have a javelin in my hand or be lacing up my speed skates, but I guess the sign means we're in the right place.

My mom has some cookie deliveries to make, but she'll be back later. I don't know if my dad is coming. I didn't ask, and my mom didn't say. I know Maya's parents definitely will be here later, and Linc's probably won't be. He said he thought they both had to work.

The competition starts in an hour. I'm nervous. The kind of nervous that if I was a girl I might say I have butterflies. But guys don't say they have butterflies, so I won't say that. Ever. It's also the kind of nervous that usually makes my stomach churn and clench. But that's not happening. Not today. I touch my grandpa's medal through my shirt to remind myself. I've got this.

"Wow. Look at all these people. I guess this is a big deal, huh?" Linc stands just inside the door of the enormous auditorium with his mouth open.

"Yeah, it's a big deal. It's a huge competition. There are schools here from all over the state. Sister Stevie told us all that," I say.

"Look at all the girls." Linc turns his head this way and that. He stops and looks at me for a minute. And he wanders off to check out the crowd, a giant duffel bag over his shoulder. He says his project is all in there. I hope it is. I also hope he remembers to set up his booth before the judges start coming around.

I look at Maya. She rolls her eyes, and we both laugh. Then I see something that causes my laugh to get stuck in my throat. It's the team from Overton Prep.

They're wearing uniforms, like they're a baseball team or something. Some of them are pushing huge containers on wheels. Others carry tubes that look like the cylinders you would pack a poster in, but they're super-sized. And they're chanting something as they walk by.

"O-O-O don't you know? We're Overton, here we go!"

At the head of the line is a short, round man with a shiny bald head. His face is red like someone who's been in the sun too long, and he's pumping his fist in the air. This must be Mr. Bitterman—Mr. Dooley's arch-nemesis.

The Overton Prep team marches past us. Maya and I stand there for a minute and then look at each other. "I'm starting to feel a little like David, but without the slingshot," says Maya.

"And they're supposed to be Goliath?" She nods. "I'm not worried," I say. "And anyway, remember—David won."

But Maya is starting to freak out. All the signs are there—hair twirling, lip biting, nervous bouncing on the balls of her feet. Somebody needs to keep cool, and it's going to have to be me.

The chanting of the Overton Prep team gets fainter as they move through the auditorium. "Come on. Let's go find where we're supposed to set up," I say.

Maya nods and follows behind me, her cello case thumping against her leg with every step. We walk past rows and rows of booths, looking for a sign that says St. Jude. Everyone else looks like they know what they're doing—like they've been here before. I wonder if we're the only new ones.

At the end of the last row we spot Sister Stevie. "Oh good, my captains are here," she says. "We have these six booths right here, and we need to start setting up. The judging starts in less than an hour." Sister Stevie seems anxious, too. She's talking so fast it's hard to keep up, and her hands are gesturing all over the place.

Rachel's presentation on the science of poetry is already set up. She has books of poetry on display and has blown up a few poems onto huge canvases—like paintings. That's the art part of it. Then she has graphs and formulas to explain the science part of it. It looks great. And so does she. She's talking to a guy who, by the way he's mooning over her, must be her boyfriend.

The other five booths are empty. Maya heaves her cello onto the table in the one on the end, so I guess that's hers. I take the one next to it. I have a giant equipment bag of my dad's filled with the stuff for my display, and my grandpa's briefcase holds all of my documentation. I unzip the bag and start pulling out all the sports equipment.

I have a basketball, a baseball and bat, golf balls, a football, and a tennis racket and ball. Then there is my mom's laptop with the presentation and a bunch of handouts on each of the specific sports. I feel pretty good about how it all turned out. I hope that feeling lasts.

Ty comes over and grabs the basketball off my table, spinning it on his finger. "This all looks pretty cool." He starts flipping through my stacks of handouts. "Hey, I shot free throws underhand at practice yesterday."

"Yeah?"

"Yeah." Ty spins the ball on his finger again, looks up at me and grins. "I made sixteen out of twenty. Coach couldn't believe it. He's making all the guys try."

"Go, granny, go!" I grin back at Ty and straighten up the stacks he just finished unstacking.

"So, hey, I kind of got you something." Ty reaches into his pocket and pulls out something about the size of an index card.

He puts the card on top of one of my stacks of statistics. When I pick it up, I see it's a holy card. Not exactly what I'd expect to get from Ty. On the front is a picture of a guy from a long time ago wearing a funny black beanie kind of hat. I flip it over. Saint Albert the Great.

"I picked him for you because he was super smart and because he's the patron saint of scientists," says Ty.

Wow.

"And I picked Saint Sebastian for me because he's the patron saint of athletes. See?" Ty flashes another holy card at me before stuffing it in his pocket.

"The way I figure it, we don't need Saint Jude so much

anymore. But you never know when you might need somebody else," he says.

"Thanks, Ty. Really." Saint Albert the Great, patron saint of scientists. That sounds good. Really good.

"Everybody at your stations. Two minutes to judging." Sister Stevie runs from one table to the next, holding onto her veil with one hand. The only table still missing its person is Linc's.

"No way. I can't believe he did this." Maya's voice is in my ear. I turn to see what she's talking about. It's Linc. And I can't believe he did this either.

"What do you think?" asks Linc. "I'm Dr. Love." He stands with his arms outstretched so that we can get the full effect. Linc is wearing what I'm guessing is one of his dad's white doctor coats and a fake pair of glasses on the end of his nose. He's taped a nametag on the chest that reads "Dr. Love" and is wearing a stethoscope with a giant construction paper heart on it.

I don't know whether to laugh or strangle him. Then he smiles his Linc smile. The one that makes it impossible to get mad at him.

I can tell the exact moment when he sees Rachel and her boyfriend. Linc's cheesy smile flickers for just a second and then comes back bigger than ever. "I'm going to teach the ladies about the science of love."

"Well, Dr. Love, judging starts soon so get moving," says Maya. She gives his stethoscope a twirl, rolls her eyes, and laughs. It looks like Dr. Love even works on Maya.

Linc starts setting up his booth and then stops and looks back at me. "Hey, Gabe, let me know if you see my mom, okay? She said she'd try to come, but you know . . ."

Our team scrambles to get ready and then Sister Stevie gathers us around for a quick pep talk and a Hail Mary. She's just wrapping up when the gong sounds—judging begins now. We all scurry to our stations like mice and wait to be evaluated. Game time.

Sister Stevie paces from one end of our collection of cubes to the other. Mr. Dooley alternates between shouting weird things like "Show 'em what you've got"—which I guess is supposed to be inspirational, and standing on his tiptoes so he can peer over the wall and spy on the Overton Prep team.

I hear him mutter something about Mr. Bitterman that would get me detention if I said it in school or grounded if I said it at home. Then he lowers himself back onto his feet and says, "Robots. They've got robots."

Maya's head spins around so fast I'm afraid she might have pulled a muscle in her neck. She locks eyes with me and mouths, "Robots?"

I shrug. It's way past too late to freak out about what Overton Prep or anyone else is doing.

I hiss, "Here come the judges. We're on."

They stop at Ty's booth first—and it's awesome. His panorama of the racetrack turned out better than I imagined it could. He has race sound effects and an actual stock car driver's helmet for the judges to check out. Some of them even try it on.

After Ty comes Maya.

"I've written out a piece of music where each note is represented by its corresponding sound frequency. Sound frequency is measured in hertz. The A note has a frequency of 440 hertz, and every other note is represented by 440 hertz multiplied by the ratio of frequencies between half tones." Maya talks fast and points at a bunch of numbers and lines with her cello bow.

The judges stand there staring at Maya for what feels like a long time. I know how they feel. She explained it to me three times, and I still don't get it.

But then Maya sits down with her cello, takes her bow, and plays the same piece of music. And she doesn't need to say anything else. The judges applaud when she's done and Maya beams. Then she looks over at me, blows her bangs out of her eyes, and gives me a look that says as clearly as words, "Don't screw up."

The judges shuffle sideways until they're in front of my display. Every one of them is looking at me. I wait for the usual panicky, stomach clenching feeling to start deep inside. But it doesn't. Not today. I look around and find the judge with the friendliest face—he looks like Santa Claus might have looked when he was younger—and I talk to him.

"Sir, what's your favorite sport?" I ask.

"Well, I used to play a lot of baseball. Still play when I get the chance," he says.

"Let me ask you this: If you were trying to hit a home-run, and you had the choice between a larger bat and a smaller bat, which would you choose?"

He looks at me and smiles. "The bigger the bat, the bigger the hit." He looks around at the other judges. "Is that right, young man?"

"Actually, no." The other judges laugh, and one nudges my Santa Claus guy in the arm. Mr. Santa Claus strokes his beard and narrows his eyes.

"A lot of people think a bigger bat is the secret to more power," I say. "But the real secret is the speed at which you move the bat. And a smaller bat allows you to move the bat faster, which lets you hit the ball farther."

"Tell me more," says Mr. Santa Claus. "I'm not convinced yet." He still looks friendly, but I don't think he's ready to admit he was wrong.

"Okay. When you hit the baseball, you want to give it as much energy as possible. The equation that determines the amount of energy something has when it's moving is $E=0.5mv^2$. Energy equals 0.5 multiplied by mass multiplied by velocity squared."

The judges, most of them anyway, are nodding. I take a deep breath and keep going.

"Since the velocity—or speed—is squared, how fast you swing the bat is more important than the size of the bat you hit it with—the mass. A smaller bat swung faster generates more energy. More energy means the ball goes farther—so, more homeruns." I smile, grab a baseball, and toss it to Mr. Santa Claus. He catches it and smiles back.

"Since you made me look bad in front of my colleagues, I'm keeping the ball," he says. "Well done."

I take the judges through the rest of my presentation and answer their questions about a lot of different sports. Two of the judges even get into an argument about granny style free throws.

Even though I know it went pretty great, I'm still glad when the judges finally move on to check out Linc's Dr. Love display. They start laughing right away so I guess it's going well. The laughs get even bigger when Cameron starts his presentation.

I haven't seen Linc in a long time. His booth was unmanned for the last ten minutes of the judging. Maya went looking for him planning to either kill him or chain him to his display, but she never found him.

Here he comes. Linc is still wearing his doctor's coat. But he's not alone. He's with a girl. A cute girl with blonde hair that bounces on her shoulders when she walks. It's obvious by the way Linc's looking at her that he thinks she's cute, too.

"Hey, Gabe, this is Chloe," says Linc.

Chloe smiles and giggles. I'm not sure why she's giggling; nothing Linc said was funny.

"Hi." I look to Linc for some direction. What's going on?

"Chloe goes to Meadowbrook. She came by my booth and really liked my presentation." Linc waggles his eyebrows.

"Yeah," says Chloe. "Linc explained all about how love works. It's fascinating."

Linc looks at me and mouths the word "woo." Then he grabs Chloe's hand and walks away. "See you," he says back over his shoulder.

I laugh. I laugh because he's Linc. And because it looks like his plan worked. One of his crazy plans to get a girl actually worked.

"Come on, Gabe, the awards ceremony is starting now," says Maya. She leads the way to where Sister Stevie, Mr. Dooley, and the rest of our team—minus Linc—are already sitting. We slide into the two seats on the end.

A woman who's so short she has to hop up onto a box to see over the podium taps the microphone to get our attention.

"It's awards time, everyone," she says. There's wild cheering around the room, and I can hear the Overton Prep team start their stupid chant again. If we can't win, I just hope they don't either.

"I'm Dr. Savannah James, head of the meteorology department here at Central Carolina." The meteorology department? Cool. "And it's my privilege to present the awards for this year's Middle School Academic Olympics. I'll be awarding medals and trophies to the teams that come in first, second and third place."

Dr. James pops up onto her tiptoes and scans the room, seeming to look at each one of us. "Here we go."

Maya's leg bounces up and down so fast it's a blur. I glance over and see Mr. Dooley's forehead vein pulsing away. Even Cameron is leaning forward in his seat, waiting to hear. It feels the way it's felt all day. We're a team. A real team.

"Third place goes to the team who really impressed me personally. They each created a different type of weather event. Congratulations, Meadowbrook Middle School."

A huge cheer goes up from the other side of the auditorium. The team from Meadowbrook—including Linc's new friend Chloe—goes running up to grab their bronze medals and trophy.

I elbow Maya. "They got third place with weather. Didn't you say weather wasn't good enough?" I'm kidding—kind of.

"They got bronze. I don't want bronze," says Maya without turning her head.

I roll my eyes, settle back, and wait to see what happens next.

"The team that was awarded the silver medal impressed the judges a great deal. This wasn't a surprise since this team impresses the judges every year. They showed us robots doing things . . ."

The rest of what Dr. James says is lost on me because I'm too busy trying to get away from Maya's super pointy finger. She jabs me in the middle of my arm over and over. "Robots? That's Overton. Gabe, Overton got silver. Do you know what this means?"

It means Overton didn't win gold. It also means that my arm might be broken or at least deeply bruised. Still,

I manage to sit up as tall as I can and lean way forward. I peek around and see everyone else is doing the same.

Dr. James pops up onto her tiptoes and smiles with her whole face. "The team that wins this year's Academic Olympic's gold showed a great deal of creativity. They showed us all a different way of looking at science." Maya makes a noise that doesn't sound human. "They made science beautiful, funny, and even showed us science's romantic side." Dr. James chuckles at her own joke. "This year's Academic Olympics gold medal goes to a team competing for the first time. Congratulations, St. Jude Academy Middle School."

Inside my head, there's no sound. No anything. Then I reach up and, right through my shirt, I feel it. My grand-pa's medal. We did it, Grandpa. We really did it. All of a sudden I can hear everything. And it's loud.

I jump out of my seat and let out a whoop of my own. We really and truly won. Wow.

Maya hasn't moved. Not at all. Sister Stevie is jumping up and down, and I see her hug Mr. Dooley at the same time he's getting clapped on the back by Mr. Bitterman.

I pull Maya up by her hand and drag her behind me as our team walks to the front of the auditorium to receive our medals. I take the first-place trophy from Dr. James. It's really big and really heavy. I turn around and hold the trophy up over my head, feeling so proud of us. So proud of myself.

Linc appears next to me. He's back in his regular clothes.

"What happened to Dr. Love?" I ask him out of the side of my mouth.

"I ran into my mom. I kind of didn't ask before I took that stuff." He looks awfully happy for a guy who just got busted. "Gabe, my mom came."

The crowd cheers for us for a long time. Above all the clapping and yelling I hear a long, loud, whistle that starts low and ends high. It's my dad's whistle. I follow the sound of the whistle and find my dad in the crowd. He's standing between my mom and Sabrina, clapping and whistling. A huge smile splits his face, and I see him elbow the man standing next to him—hard. He points to me, and I can read his lips from here.

"That's my son."

About the Author

Marilee Haynes lives with her husband and three young children just outside Charlotte, North Carolina. A full-time stay-at-home mom, she writes middle-grade fiction in stolen quiet moments (in other words, when everyone else is asleep). This is her first novel.

Catholic Fiction

Pauline Teen brings you books you'll love!
We promise you stories that:

- ✍ make you laugh—and sometimes cry

- ✍ make you think and help you dream

- ✍ let you explore the real world

At Pauline, we love a good story and the long
tradition of Christian fiction.* Our books are fun
to read. Plus, they help you to engage your faith
by accepting who you are *here and now* while
inspiring you to recognize who God *calls you to
become*.

*Think of classics like *The Hobbit, The Chronicles of Narnia,
A Christmas Carol, Ben Hur,* and *The Man Who Was Thursday.*

Who: The Daughters of St. Paul

What: Pauline Teen—linking your life to Jesus Christ and his Church

When: 24/7

Where: All over the world and on www.pauline.org

Why: Because our life-long passion is to witness to God's amazing love for all people!

How: Inspiring lives of holiness through: Apps, digital media, concerts, websites, social media, videos, blogs, books, music albums, radio, media literacy, DVDs, ebooks, store, conferences, bookfairs, parish exhibits, personal contact, illustration, vocation talks, writing, editing

auline
BOOKS & MEDIA

The Daughters of St. Paul operate book and media centers at the following addresses. Visit, call or write the one nearest you today, or find us at www.pauline.org

CALIFORNIA
3908 Sepulveda Blvd, Culver City, CA 90230   310-397-8676
935 Brewster Avenue, Redwood City, CA 94063   650-369-4230
5945 Balboa Avenue, San Diego, CA 92111   858-565-9181

FLORIDA
145 S.W. 107th Avenue, Miami, FL 33174   305-559-6715

HAWAII
1143 Bishop Street, Honolulu, HI 96813   808-521-2731
Neighbor Islands call: 866-521-2731

ILLINOIS
172 North Michigan Avenue, Chicago, IL 60601   312-346-4228

LOUISIANA
4403 Veterans Memorial Blvd, Metairie, LA 70006   504-887-7631

MASSACHUSETTS
885 Providence Hwy, Dedham, MA 02026   781-326-5385

MISSOURI
9804 Watson Road, St. Louis, MO 63126   314-965-3512

NEW YORK
64 West 38th Street, New York, NY 10018   212-754-1110

PENNSYLVANIA
Philadelphia—relocating   215-676-9494

SOUTH CAROLINA
243 King Street, Charleston, SC 29401   843-577-0175

VIRGINIA
1025 King Street, Alexandria, VA 22314   703-549-3806

CANADA
3022 Dufferin Street, Toronto, ON M6B 3T5   416-781-9131